TRAITOR!

▽ ▽ ▽ ▽

The heat wave followed the blast itself, and Stone felt a rush of fifty-mile-per-hour superheated wind rush right over his back as if he were lying in front of a blast furnace. Then there was a terrible screaming. The pods who had been waiting to ambush him were all human torches now...

Stone heard sounds behind him from out of the flame-spattered darkness. And as three figures came into view, Stone knew he'd just gone from the fire into something much worse. For coming at him with a vengeance in their respective eyes were Guru Yasgar, seated atop a raging tusked elephant, and Excaliber, the traitor, running alongside a rampaging giant. Stone's own, fierce-toothed pit bull dog, looked like he wanted the first piece of flesh from the Last Ranger!

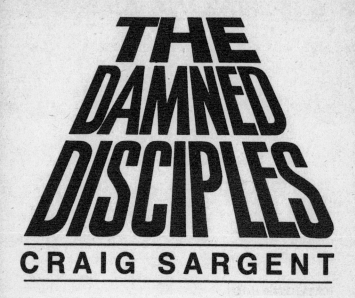

THE DAMNED DISCIPLES

CRAIG SARGENT

POPULAR LIBRARY

An Imprint of Warner Books, Inc.

A Warner Communications Company

POPULAR LIBRARY EDITION

Popular Library books are published by
Warner Books, Inc.
666 Fifth Avenue
New York, N.Y. 10103

 A Warner Communications Company

Printed in the United States of America

First Printing: October, 1988

10 9 8 7 6 5 4 3 2 1

PROLOGUE

She was brought into the room stark naked. It was part of the "cleansing" process to break them down, to humiliate them, make them feel ashamed. For shame, and its sister—guilt—were how they broke minds, how they reached inside and rearranged things to their liking. Six men wearing demonic masks and long black flowing robes sat atop high wooden chairs, thrones almost, with dark hideous carvings of snakes and demons undulating up and down their sides. With the robes and masks covering them, only the men's fingers, long and pale, which stretched out on the armrests on each side of them—and the twin pools of reflecting light that were their eyes—could be seen within their engulfing hoods. They hardly looked human.

Two strapping men wearing long brown robes and with police nightsticks strapped to their sides dragged the woman into the room holding her up under each arm. For she was resistant, to say the least, terrified, trembling and crying at every step. They half carried her to a red circle about four feet wide painted on the floor and placed her in the absolute center of it. Then they stood back so they were outside the circle.

The woman was beautiful. Even with her tear-streaked dirty face, her unwashed body that stood without a stitch of clothing before the robed ones. She looked like a living sculpture of female perfection with her upturned breasts, slim waist, and rounded hips that seemed to curve into another dimension and then back again. And the blond patch of fur between her legs, which she covered with one hand while the other tried to shield her firm young breasts from view. The tears kept running down her face in fear—and shame.

But the men who looked onto her nakedness were too old, too dried up, without enough of the juices of life left within them to find even the slightest bit of desirability in such a nubile young paragon of femininity. They no longer felt such things as desire, at least desires of the normal kind—to touch, kiss, hold—the things that men—and women—dream of. Their dreams were darker by far, without a trace of warmth or life. Dreams only of total submission, total control, total pain. The making of that which was human into something different.

"Do not cry, child," one of the robed voices spoke, his masked face just a shadow within the shadowed hood. And even as the words were spoken, she became a thousand times more frightened. For they were words that a skeleton might speak, like bones cracking together. There was no warmth in the voice, just the cold mechanical tones of something that was dead inside.

"Do not fear us, child," another voice spoke up. "We are here to make you whole, make you perfect." A hand rose up from out of the dark sleeve and her trembling increased—for the hand seemed to be without flesh, so long, so white were its fingers, so flat and narrow its palm. The finger pointed at her.

"You are chosen to be one of us. To be one of the Perfect Ones, one of the Disciples of the Perfect Aura. This is a great honor." The rest of them cackled beneath their black hoods, the sound of dry leathery tongues rasping against bone, echoing through the room.

"We are the Perfect Ones. Unlike human beings, who are confused and imperfect, we are completed—and perfect.

We are without prejudices, without any of the thousand failings of mankind. We are the Perfect Ones."

"The Perfect Ones," the other five echoed in.

"To be Perfect—is to be without fear," the head man said, his eyes like red lasers inside his hood. He was the only one with such orbs, which in the gray light of the room, glowed bloodred. "That is what makes the human mind imperfect—fear. Do you understand?"

"Y--yes," the woman stuttered, her throat catching even as she talked. "I'm afraid. Very afraid." She began crying again. "Please—let me go. I'll just leave and—" Leathery laughter met her pleas.

"No, no, there is no leaving from here," the High Priest said with the firmness of a noose snapping closed around a throat. "But do not fear, child." He rose up from his center chair and he seemed to be a giant to the woman, whose heart began beating even faster, whose tears began flowing down like an unstoppable stream. "We are here to *help* you. To take all these feelings of fear out of you—and give you peace for the first time in your life. You must just give yourself to us. All that you are."

"Give yourself to us," the others echoed from beneath their black hoods.

"You must give up the illusory idea of being a single individual. For it is *this* which gives people pain—trying to separate themselves from the herd, trying to be an individual when there can only be peace in the group. In the Perfect Whole."

"Peace in the group," the hooded figures hissed back. And now they all rose up and stepped down from their chairs and walked out to the wooden floor around her. The woman's heart began beating so rapidly that her chest could be seen moving. She would have tried to run right to the window and jump out—even to her death—anything would have been better than these "men." But she couldn't move an inch. She was paralyzed with her fear, as if curare had been injected into her muscles and not one would move. And they knew about that—the six hooded ones—the six

Priests of the Perfect Aura. They knew that fear made people lose all control, made them screaming animals without a vestige of pride or courage.

They formed a circle and began moving around her. A coat of sweat covered her naked flesh to join the flowing river of her eyes as adrenaline surged through her. As they moved, the long black robes began spinning out around them and incomprehensible sounds emerged from within. They all seemed much larger than life, the robes rising seven feet or more above the red wooden floor. And with the material flaring out around them, even their shapes seemed to change. It was hard to see them, and she was beginning to wonder if they were even men.

As they moved, they began to chant a strange guttural language. From the very dawn of time, animal sounds and clicks, tongues scraping across teeth, the language of the creatures who had become men—but were not yet men. And as the "song" emerged from their hidden lips, drums began beating around her, deep resonant sounds that were like rumbles of thunder and vibrated through her very bones as if she were in an earthquake.

Then they were going faster and the drums were rising in volume and tempo until she thought her ears would shatter from the noise. And they were spinning around her like six tops gone mad, their black robes now wide around them like the twirling skirts of gypsy dancers. And suddenly, as they hit cruising speed, they pulled out objects from inside their thick cotton robes and held them out, waving and shaking the things as they circled.

She screamed now. The paralysis at least left her lips for a few moments. And her hands flew up over her face as she totally forgot that she had been covering her more personal areas. She kept screaming. For the things they were holding out were organ parts of the human body. One held an eyeball out at the end of its dripping tendrils, shaking the thing like a rattle every time he passed around her. Another held a human arm, hand, fingers and all, and gripped it by the open arm wound, stabbing it in her direction so that fingers almost touched her face each time he ran by. One waved a heart, another gripped a dried human brain though it kept disintegrating within his bony fingers. Another a male sex organ, huge and dried out, like some long dead snake, whipping it toward her skull like a bludgeon. And the sixth, the Head Priest—the Transformer, she saw, as he made his turn—was holding an entire human head, eyes opened, staring at her, tongue hanging sideways out of its mouth as dried blood coated the worm-infested lips like lipstick to give it a little class. They whirled faster and faster until it was all just a blur and she didn't even realize she was screaming without stop.

The hands snapped out their dead objects and began making contact with her as they whirled in a circle just a yard or so out from her naked, shaking body. She covered her face and eyes with her hands, like a child trying to hide from nightmares beneath the blankets. But these nightmares weren't going away.

Suddenly they stopped, and the drums, too, ceased in midbeat. After a few moments she dared open her eyes just a fraction of an inch and peered through the shielding hands. One of the underlings in brownish-red robe was carrying in a platter with a silver cover over it, like some sort of Foie gras at a four-star restaurant—when there had been such things. He carried it to the Head Priest, who put his skull down and, opening both arms wide, addressed her solemnly.

"*Now* you will go through fear, live fear, become fear. And when you emerge on the other side—you will no longer live *in* fear. You will be beyond it. I am the Transformer. I shall make you as we are. Give yourself up, little one, there is nothing to save. There is no self."

"*There is no self,*" the others chanted loudly.

He lifted the silver cover, and she gasped. Inside, on a shining silver tray with all kinds of strange symbols and designs etched into its surface, was a human skull—and it was filled with liquid that danced and shimmered gold even in the shadowy grayness.

"The Liquid of Purification," the Head Priest said with reverence. "The Golden Elixir. Drink." He lifted the skull to her lips, and she screamed again and stepped back. Or tried to—for two guards were right there behind her and by merely placing their bodies in the right spot they locked her in place so she couldn't move.

"Drink, drink," they screamed. The High Priest stepped forward, clamped an iron hand around her head, and pulled it backward. Then he forced some of the liquid from the skull into her mouth.

It burned, burned horribly, and she coughed and gagged and spat up half of it. But enough had gotten in to satisfy the pourer, and he stepped back, putting the skull back onto the platter. The guard walked off slowly, each step exaggerated, ritualized.

"There. Isn't that better already?" The Transformer asked with a lying fatherly concern. "The Golden Elixir you have drunk—it will help you to get through the barrier of fear. Because it will exaggerate that fear a thousandfold. So you will have no way of resisting any longer. Give in, child, give in. All will be without pain soon."

The liquid hurt her mouth and throat and everything it touched on the way down. Whatever it was, it worked fast. For the woman had hardly stopped coughing, her whole chin soaked in the sticky spittle, when everything began getting weird. The six men around her began elongating and shrinking, almost melting before her as if they were made of clouds, not flesh. She was so dizzy she could hardly stand up, but the guards wouldn't let her fall.

A box was carried into the room accompanied by the beating of the drums. It was as if she were in a fun house, where everything changed, everything was seen through a distorting mirror. And it was all twisted and horrible. And though she didn't really know what was going on, she knew somehow that she was drugged. And that things were just going to get worse.

"IITTTT ISSSSSS DDEEEEEEATTHHH WEEEEE FFEEEAARRR," the High Priest was saying, though his words sounded crazy, like a record on slow speed, everything deep and trembling.

"*DEEAAATTTHHH WEEEE FEEEAARR,*" the others chanted back.

"*SOOOO IIITTT IISSSS DEEAATHHH WEEEE MUUUUST LEEARNN TOOO LOOOVVVE.*"

"*WEEEE LOOOVEEE DEATTTHH!*" the others chanted.

The pine box was placed on the floor by the four men who were holding it and the top was opened. Inside was a corpse, recently departed. It couldn't have been more than a week old, since much of its flesh was still there. But it had had plenty of time to rot, too. The features of the face were all blended together like a child's finger painting. The flesh was bloated and white, with worms and bugs eating their way through little tunnels and canyons within. The whole thing crawled with vermin, lice, spiders, slugs, fungi, and molds.

She screamed again. And this time under the influence of the dozen or so mind-altering drugs that were mixed into the Elixir, the scream was like a waterfall and seemed to take her into another world, another dimension, where she was blind and deaf, and something was pressing all around her, squeezing her in.

And when she opened her eyes again as the scream stopped for an instant, she saw that they were in fact touching her—pushing her down into the box in which slept the moldering dead one. She was thrown right on top of the rotting mess so that bugs and worms scampered back into the innards. She began screaming again—so hard that she split her lips as her teeth bit through. The motion of the guards' push made the corpse thing whip its arms up around her so it held her in an embrace. Its devil's bad dream of a face, with a centipede staring right out at her through one of the green-slimed eyeholes, looked up at her and seemed to wink. Then the leathery brown lips twisted back as ants came out of each corner of the mouth searching for more food for their colony in the guts of the dead creature.

The underlings nailed the top back down right above her back, so she was wedged down even farther into the "man." It pressed close against her like an ardent, horny, even anxious, lover. And as the cold decomposing arms wrapped around as though they'd just never let go, its swamp of a face pressed ever closer—the hard lips smacking at her as if trying to kiss her, the bugs inside clacking their mandibles as if whispering sweet nothings. Through the long black night, the unmoving cold tried to make love to the screaming warm.

ONE

The battle-scarred rat stood up on its hind legs and sniffed at the wind. There was meat ahead. It could smell the warm-blooded creatures not far off. Human meat. It knew the smell. It had, after all, been a hunter, the leader of the pack for two years now, a long, long time in rat linealogy. And though not many, they had taken humans down, had survived their weapons—and eaten them.

It was the toughest of them, with its nearly two-foot-long body, a good thirty pounds of savage fury contained within a shimmering black pelt slashed here and there with scars and gouges—and fangs that seemed too big for its mouth, curving out long and ivory white like canines. The lingering radiation of the nukes that had gone off years before nearby had done a little twisting and rearranging of chromosomes. So that what was once a nuisance, a vermin, a pest, was now a horror. Something from a nightmare on the coldest of winter eves.

Its blood-coated whiskers twitched in the sharp morning breeze. It had eaten already; it and its pack had killed a wounded stag they'd come across in the forest. It hadn't been able to run fast enough and had fallen beneath their vicious onslaught. It was ripped to shreds and eaten within minutes, so that not a trace of it remained. Not even the

bones. That was only hours before. But it was a mere snack.
There were many in the pack, many mouths to be fed. The
Leader turned and surveyed its army, which scampered
around and over each other behind it. Thousands of them,
stretching off in a rough column nearly a hundred yards
long, twenty yards wide. It looked at them with its one good
eye; the other, bitten in half long ago by a rival male now
deceased, had shrunken down to the size of a shriveled rai-
sin, black and hard like a fragment of coal. The ripped and
torn creature inspired fear in even the largest of the other
rats, who dared not look straight into the scarred, misshapen
face.

Its right eye worked just fine. The Leader stood up on a
rock so that it was a good five feet above the squealing
masses, always almost out of control—almost. But under its
direction they moved like an army, letting nothing stand in
their way. When it was gone . . . who could say. But such
things rats didn't worry about. Just the next meal. For as the
Russian czar had learned in the Revolution of 1918, "a lack
of bread to eat is the fire of revolution." The Leader was
trapped too. It had to feed them all, make sure the ravenous
hordes didn't turn—on him.

The Leader made motions with his paws, commanding
the army of rats, brown and black and gray, sleek and fanged
with long tails dragging behind them, into two flanks. He
would scout straight up the center, and when he called, they
knew to come. He was the general. His strategies had
worked time and time again. Food was the reward they got
in return for their loyalty, their willingness to fight, to die for
the Leader. He delivered. And it was eating time. Bring on
the hot stuff. The human meat that tasted so sweet. A rat's
greatest delicacy.

Martin Stone walked down the deer path along the edge
of some thick woods supporting himself on a homemade
crutch fashioned from a V-topped branch, cursing every step
of the way.

"Fuck, shit, piss. Goddamn leg—can't even walk or do

anything anymore. A man can't even trust his own body parts—who the hell can he trust? I ask you fucking that." Though he didn't actually address the leg, keeping his eyes ahead looking for groundhog and snake holes, as he had already fallen twice in the last hour and didn't feel like doing it again. But the leg damn well knew who he was talking to. Ever since he had broken it in a fall two weeks before, it had been causing him all kinds of trouble. First it had swollen up to the size of a balloon. Then, with herbs and cauterizing it and setting it with a splint, it had seemed to go down again. He had thought maybe it was actually going to heal, and everything would be all right.

Yeah, right. Only, the leg was swollen again, and a very strange color along the whole side of his thigh. He could feel a pounding in his heart—and knew he was getting blood poisoning. Stone had been having hallucinations for the last few hours. Things crawling along the edges of the woods, always just out of his sight. It wasn't that far to the bunker. He just had to make it to his late father's mountain retreat, built into the side of a mountain, and equipped with the most modern equipment, computers, even medical supplies. Somehow he would have to treat himself, cut the leg open and . . . But he'd worry about that later. First he had to even try to stagger the next five miles to the mountain at the north end of Estes National Park in northern Colorado—then go straight up the side of the thing for another mile or two. . . . He prayed he had enough left in him to make it. He was on his last leg.

There was a low growl at his feet, and Stone looked down as he almost tripped over the furred shaped that kept walking back and forth in front of him.

"Watch it, dog, will you, for Christ's sake," Stone muttered, in no mood for even the slightest bit of bullshit on a cold, painful morning like this one was turning out to be. He looked down and into the almond-shaped eyes of the ninety-pound pit bull that was trotting along looking up. It appeared to be pissed off as hell, its face all squinched up and glaring at Stone as if to say, "We haven't eaten diddly-shit beyond some acorns and a few berries in the last twelve hours. Dogs can be assholes too." Or something like that.

"We'll be there soon fucking enough," the fighting terrier's human companion snapped down. "Cool it, dog! You're supposed to be man's best friend—not his biggest hassle. Just chill out, food hound. Cripples don't need tripping." The dog growled under its breath and looked away disgustedly, as if it might catch a glimpse of something edible in the woods. It was never meaner than when traveling on an empty stomach, like a fighter without sex for a month before the big bout. The lack of chewable substance in its jaws sent the pit bull into a deep, dark, and brooding depression. Chow Boy better not get too close to him, that's all the dog had to say about the subject.

But suddenly all the arguing and snapping at one another like an ancient married couple was irrelevant. Excaliber sensed them first, stopping suddenly in his tracks, just a few feet ahead of Stone, so the human nearly toppled over the top of the dog. Stone started to curse up a storm, and raised his crutch ready to smack the canine a good stiff one right on the flank, when he saw that Excaliber was set in full attack posture, pointing back in the direction they had just come from. Stone knew the animal would never go into fighting mode against *him*, no matter how snappy their little argument. So he shut up and turned slowly around, supporting himself on the branch.

"Shit-coated Crispies," Stone muttered under his breath, not even aware he had said the words. He didn't like what he saw. Not one fucking bit. Rats. An army of them, making the terrain just a blanket of brown and black swarming little bodies with way too many and too big teeth for their foot-and-a-half- to two-foot-long frames. And they were closing in from both sides fast, the forward ranks only a hundred yards or so away. Just ahead of the advancing vermin army came several gophers and a snake or two, all scared up by the meat-eating procession that chewed down everything that got in its way. Though the invasion of claws and snapping jaws was clearly after the pink stuff. And that meant one

Martin Stone. Which, as he thought not too hard about it, he realized was him.

Stone shook his head hard seeing that he was half hypnotized by the horror show coming in fast. He didn't have time to be falling into spaceland right now—or he was going to be meeting a lot of hungry mouths within about three seconds. Bracing himself on the branch crutch that was under his left armpit, Stone whipped the shotgun he had snatched from an encampment of dead cannibals—whom he had put in that state—and swung it around in front of him. The pit bull was snarling now, its jaws wide as it pulled back, its tail just touching Stone's leg—so it knew its back was covered. At least Chow Boy better see that it *was* covered. The dog didn't like the gray skulking shapes that ran along on fast little claws one fucking bit. Shivers ran along its spine like dirty waves at Coney Island Beach.

"Come on," Stone screamed as his slow-witted brain realized they were being surrounded. Already they were blocked on three sides; only the field directly ahead was not yet blanketed with the squirming little bodies crying out in squeaking high-pitched commands to one another. "Let's move it, dog. And I mean fucking pronto!" He started ahead, lurching along on the crutch as he gripped the shotgun hard so it wouldn't fall out. Suddenly the brown sea of rats came rushing in from every side—even ahead—and Stone realized they had been successfully cut off. He dropped the shotgun arm down as low as he could hold it and still keep moving, stumbling, half falling ahead. He pulled the trigger and the 12-gauge autofire slammed back in his hands, threatening to pull him backward. But it did a hell of a lot worse to the wall of gray and brown straight ahead. The shot left the muzzle only about six inches above the ground—and spread out a good ten feet before it met vermin flesh coming in. The steel pellets got the better of the smashup, and a whole slew of rats went flying off in bloody spirals as a pathway was cleared right through the living swarm.

As Stone stumbled forward he could sense the rats coming and snapping at his boots, trying to climb up him. But Excaliber met them face to face, jaw to jaw, tooth to snapping tooth. Only, his were bigger, faster, and meaner. For as one would leap up toward the charging pair, the pit bull would catch it in midair like some mutt out in the backyard catching a hot dog fresh off the family grill. With a single snap the pit bull spat them out again, moving, never stopping. He took care of those that charged toward Stone's legs as well, ripping them right off the Chow Boy's pants as they tried to scamper up and get some fang into his flesh. In seconds the pit bull had disposed of a dozen, leaving their spurting corpses behind, which others of the pack stopped and began chewing on. A meal on the run was always a happy occurrence.

Seeing that the dog was taking care of business down below, Stone turned his attention to their forward escape route, their *only* escape route. And it'd better be fast, he could see as he did a quick 180-degree scan without breaking his uneven half-run, for within twenty or thirty seconds the main bulk of the rat army would be upon them—and that, no matter how wildly they fought, would be that.

He aimed the shotgun again, holding it down as low as he could, as if he were reaching for the ground, and pulled the trigger. The reason he had grabbed this particular blunderbuss over other, higher-quality, firepower was just for the autoeject and instant refire mode. It meant he could keep pulling at the damn thing with just one hand. The second shell sent out a hailstorm of pellets from the smoking muzzle. And another forty or so rats who thought they were about to be in culinary heaven were suddenly nothing more that flopping dead meat, their dark pelts saturated with red, their own brothers and sisters already chewing on their still-feeling flesh.

Suddenly Stone sensed a shape coming up at him from the left and turned his head just in time to see the biggest goddamn rat he had ever laid eyes on—a good two feet plus—launch itself and come toward him, its jaws fully extended like something Cape Kennedy might have once launched to scare the shit out of the rest of the universe. Somehow Stone twisted his whole body and ripped the shotgun up trying to get a bead on the thing, which was closing in on his very eyeballs. He could count the whiskers on the ugly one-eyed face. He pulled the trigger and shifted the crutch around fast to stop himself from going down from the recoil.

The rat took the full load of shot from a distance of two feet. The creature disintegrated in the air, like a balloon that had popped, a balloon filled with blood and slime that filled the air around Stone with a slick red spray that lingered like a mist. But he wasn't counting the drops. Swinging the shotgun around, he let off two more blasts and then got to full, stumbling gallop in seconds. Another wave of little flesheaters went flying off like rag dolls painted red, and Stone and the dog waded right through and over the twitching bodies, nearly falling and slipping in the pools of wet fur, the puddles of hot blood.

Still, for all the heroics and sound and fury, Stone knew they needed a miracle. As he scouted ahead, looking around desperately for he didn't know what, he saw a chasm in the earth—a fissure, glacially created. It formed a long jagged crack in the earth a good six feet wide and nearly a quarter-mile long. If miracles were needed, this was looking like it might be in the right department. Excaliber saw it too, and he barked hard at Stone twice, signaling him to make sure the Chow Boy had seen it. The canine knew that the human could get a little fog-headed at times.

Stone fired twice more and then, when he fired a third time, felt a click. Empty. He had more shells in the pack on his back, but somehow he didn't think the rodent army was going to allow him to take a look. The last two volleys of death-dealing lead carved out a pathway through the rats right to the edge of the rock fissure. Stone and the pit bull tore through the bloody debris of violently shaking corpses. Excaliber got up to full running speed and took off without looking down. In an instant the animal had soared over the fissure and landed on the far side. He turned and, seeing that

Stone wasn't there, looked back across the gap and let out with a long howl, throwing his head back, as if to say, "Oh shit, man, you in trouble again?"

Stone's crutch caught at the last instant, just before he was about to send himself flying into space. He nearly fell into the deep fissure, seeing its jagged rock walls disappear below into darkness. The damn thing went all the fucking way to the center of the earth, for all he knew. But he caught himself at the last instant with his hands and knees, having to pull back with all his strength to stop himself from shooting over the side.

But out of the frying pan and into the fucking fire. For the rats were closing in as if he'd just said something very bad about their mothers—death in every snarling snout, every beady eye. He scrambled to his feet, stepped back about two yards from the edge, and, knowing he wouldn't have time for much of a start, launched himself forward. Stone had time to take two steps and then leap up with his good leg. At the same instant he pushed down hard with both arms against the crutch with everything he had, trying to use it as an instant pole vault stick to get some leverage.

It half worked. He went shooting off the edge just as a dozen rats launched themselves straight at his departing body, not wanting the meal to get away. The force of the takeoff had enough momentum—but it also twisted him around sideways so that as he flew over the dark chasm Stone was looking almost upside down at the thing. And even as he soared he could feel that he had taken along some visitors for the ride—gnawing little teeth began stabbing into him here and there. He'd worry about them later—if there was a later.

Suddenly the other side of the fissure was upon him and Stone managed to twist his body all the way around, coming down on his rib cage. He hit at chest level, slamming hard with all the air being forced out of him. For a second he swore he was going to fall backward right into the hole. But he sent out a burst of strength into his arms and hands that clawed and ripped at the dirt and rocks and somehow began pulling him up. Even as he rose up over the side, Stone felt the bites of the airborne pals. But Excaliber was on them in a flash, barking and snarling up a storm as he saw the ugly critters. He snapped out at Stone three times—and threw three bleeding bodies right over the side of the chasm, where they ricocheted back and forth all the way down with wet sounds like billiard balls dipped in blood.

Stone rolled back as he heard the pit bull barking and standing in full fighting stance, its jaws wide, its eyes little slits for protection. He saw a whole front wave of rats come flying toward the far side of the fissure and—jump. And though they gave it a damn good try and some of them nearly *did* make it, not one did. Twenty more went hurtling down into the darkness, sending up a chorus of squeaks.

Seeing that the army, as fierce and furious as they were, couldn't touch them, Stone and the pit bull relaxed slightly, the dog letting his puffed-out fur come down, his head pop out from its neck a little farther from the defensive turtlelike posture it had been in. Stone just tried to let his double-timing heart slow down a little, or he'd be looking for a pacemaker in the ruins of the malls. Yet another wave of the bastards came tearing right at the side and another dozen or so of the bravest, a.k.a. "stupidest," also gave it the old rodent try. With equal nonsuccess. And more of the furry bodies went slamming all the way down so that they left a little remembrance of themselves at each stop along the way.

But at last, even the slow-witted vermin realized that they were getting nowhere fast and were going to lose a lot more of their dues-paying membership if this kept up. They stopped. Hundreds of them gathered just yards away from Stone and screamed and clawed at the air, as if they were imagining in great detail what it would be like to sink their fangs into his flesh. Those in the back ranks began eating their fallen comrades, so nicely diced up and cut into little bite-sized pieces by the shotgun blasts. Stone and the bull terrier could hear the slurping sounds all along the death field. Not wanting to miss out on the feast, the front battle ranks broke off pursuit and turned away from the human and the dog, who stared back with disgusted eyes. The squealing carnivores began fighting viciously over the remains of their late relatives. They tore around the charnel grounds, their mouths like vacuum cleaners, just fractions of an inch above the red-soaked ground, gobbling down everything that wasn't nailed down.

TWO

The first thousand feet up the side of the mountain atop which the bunker had been built wasn't bad at all. Stone would ordinarily have gone all the way around the far side of the mountain, where a winding road led all the way to the top. It was an extra two hours by motorcycle. Only, he didn't have a bike anymore—which meant it was an extra two *days* or more on a single leg. Stone knew he didn't have that much time. His leg was too infected, the fever in his body rising by the hour. Either he made it up to the 12,000-foot summit from the base of about 8,000—where he was now—or it would all pretty much be over. He had to try. If he fell, at least it would be fast.

Still, that was all theoretical. For when he stopped and rested on an outcropping, and looked down, Stone saw that he was already far up. Really far. He would drop thousands of feet before being slammed to bloody pulp on the rocks below. He gulped hard and vowed not to look again. He never had been good with heights. And he saw that it was getting harder, rapidly. Whereas he had pretty much been hopping around from ledge to ledge, now it grew steeper. To make his way up, he had to search for handholds, small cracks, little outcroppings hardly wider than half a telephone booth.

The dog, of course, was a regular fucking mountain goat, hopping all over the damn place and barking back down, inquiring what the hell was taking Stone so long. If showing off was a sin, then the pit bull was going straight to hell when the shit hit the fan. Stone would vouch for that. Still, the very fact that the dog *was* able to climb up ahead of him, go up the side of what seemed like Mount Everest, at least showed him that it could be done. And the sheer determination not to let himself be bested by a damn dog gave him some driving mental motivation as well. At any rate, he was pulling himself up using almost all arm strength after a while, resting here and there, then getting up another twenty, thirty feet and having to stop again.

After a while it became too hard even for that, though the pit bull seemed able to keep on so that when Stone looked up the animal was already a good four hundred feet ahead of him and tearing up the steep slope as if he was on flatland. Stone stopped on a decent-size outcropping and took a good look ahead to scout out any holds. It was getting *much* worse. He needed something beyond hands—needed a whole fucking mountain-climbing outfit, with ropes and all. Suddenly he had an idea. It was ridiculous, impossible, insane. But maybe it would work. Stone took off the pack he had been carrying, filled with supplies he had gathered from the dead cannibal village. He didn't need them now. If he made it to the bunker, there were plenty more supplies. If not . . .

Throwing cans, matches, and various things over the side, Stone took the hunting knife he had ripped off from a corpse and began slicing up the thick U.S. Army canvas rucksack, circa 1975. He took the metal clasps off the thing and reattached them to a single long piece of webbing that, by cutting in two, Stone extended to nearly twelve feet. He secured the clasps to one end, tying them together, and then bent their stiff clasps back, having to bang them against a rock. But after a few minutes he had fashioned something that at least resembled a hook on the end of a rope. He threw the hook end up; it took five tries before it seemed to catch on to a fissure in the sheer granite wall above.

Now was better than yesterday, though he wouldn't have minded waiting for tomorrow, Stone thought glumly to himself as he started hoisting himself right up the side. After stretching out a little as the thick canvas material gave but didn't break, and hearing the metal hooks above squeak and bend, Stone found that the contraption held. He pulled himself keeping his body close against the rock, so that he wouldn't somehow pull outward and dislodge the hooks from their resting place. Slowly he dragged himself the twelve feet, like a slug as flat as a pancake against the hard surface.

Stone reached the hook, took it out, and then scouted farther up. There—an almost V-shaped set of boulders. If he could get it between them. This time it took only three tries.

"See—getting good already," Stone lauded himself, not even daring to look down anymore, as he realized that although this method might work for going up, there was no way in hell it would do so for the reverse. This was a one-way trip. Top floor, express elevator, no stops—Men's Life and Death Department. Thank you. Stone tried the green strap, letting his weight pull hard on it. The whole setup seemed to be holding. He could hear the pit bull barking far above him now as if in the clouds, luring him on knowing it would piss Chow Boy off with its gloating and barking up a fucking storm.

Stone pulled hard and rose up off the ledge. This time it was a little easier as he dragged himself up hand over hand to the hook end. It was just a matter of going slow, blending into the mountain. He remembered his father, Major Clayton Stone, telling him something, when he had been describing his years fighting in the jungles.

"Wherever you are, Martin, blend in with your terrain. Hug it like a piece of grass, surround it like a jungle vine. But become part of it. In harmony with it. Then it will let you pass through it." Like all advice, it was sure as hell a lot easier to want to carry out than to actually do so. But Stone mumbled a few prayers to the mountain, pretended he was just a growth of branches just moving along the thing. Perfect harmony. And thus he ascended the very face of Estes Mountain, moving faster as he gained confidence.

Stone was getting the hang of it, and his eyes getting better at picking out the small cracks that meant a possible anchoring station for his gear, when suddenly he heard a sound right in front of his face and a fluttering of wings. He stopped and pushed aside what he thought had been a purple-leafed bush growing right out of the side of the mountain. Behind the bush was a nest. And three small fluffy birds sat in the mound of twigs and vine, chirping up a storm as their hooked beaks opened and closed like snapping turtles.

Stone's face broke into a broad smile in spite of his fear and precarious position. The damn things were cute as hell as they flopped around like fluffy little stuffed toys, hardly real, too fucking cute for words. At least, two of them were —for Stone suddenly got a glimpse of the third one, hidden in the back beneath some straw. And this was one that wasn't so cute. Something had gone wrong. He had been seeing more of them now. Mutations. The radiation left by the bombs that had been dropped five years before—the reason he and his family had been rushed to the shelter by his father. Radiation damage sometimes took a generation— even two—before it made itself fully felt. They had learned that at Hiroshima. And the twisted scaly thing, with a face like a little demon that hissed up at him, definitely had its genes twisted around some way. It sure as hell wasn't a normal chick. But he suddenly had a hell of a lot more to worry about than the future of the eagle species. He heard a flap of wings, a loud cawing sound, and then a shadow covered his entire body. Stone turned, startled, wondering what the hell could be shadowing him 11,000 feet up. The fucking mother. She was huge—and mean. The great curved beak came snapping at him and Stone was barely able to duck out of the way as the jaws slashed at his face. He threw the hook up and mercifully caught it on the first try, pulling himself without even testing it.

The eagle's talons came slashing at his back as the bird thought he was reaching farther into the nest. Stone raised himself, his arms moving like little steam pistons as they pulled him quickly into the sky. The talons of the enraged bird slashed down the back of his jacket, which fortunately for Stone was a thick leather biker jacket that he had snatched from a dead soul who didn't need it anymore. And even that, thick enough to take rolls from a bike at sixty miles per hour, began turning to tatters from the eagles' relentless blurred assault.

Now that Stone was above the nest and not any immediate threat to it, the bird suddenly halted its attack. The great golden and white feathered carnivore hovered above the hatchlings flapping its yard-wide wings and counting them with its crystal eyes—even the scaly one, which it didn't quite know what to make of yet but was going to raise along with the other three. They were unharmed. Its trained eye detected no wounds, no red along the puffy white down. The creature on the mountainside hadn't had a chance to eat them. The eagle cawed twice to the chicks, which set them hopping about and opening and closing their mouths like waste-disposal units set on fast.

The bird swung its wide wings together and took off right up the side of the mountain so that within a second it was just behind Stone's head again and looking hard at what the struggling human's plans were.

"Fuck off bird, will you!" Stone screamed out, his voice bouncing off the jagged mica-flecked rocks that scraped at his chest and face as he pulled himself up. "I'm gone, I'm history. Go give some fucking upchuck to juniors down there, okay?" He reached the anchor spot and ripped the hooks out without even daring to turn his head around. He could sense that the bird was just inches behind him, could feel it as the flapping wings blew a strong breeze over him, ruffling his hair as if he were in a storm.

But the eagle, though it cawed at him with little stinging

messages to get the hell out of there, and clawed at the air just a yard or so behind him to show what it could do if it wanted to, seemed content to let Stone go. Which was fine with Stone. The bird could have the whole fucking mountainside. If he ever made it to the top, he'd never even *look* at the hellish slope again. But the adrenaline that surged through his system from the attack gave him pently of energy to climb the remaining three hundred feet. It took only an hour and a half. Which was pretty amazing for a one legged man.

THREE

It took only a few more minutes for Stone to reach the slope into which the bunker had been built. The major had spared no expense when it came to protecting his family. As the head of one of the country's most successful munitions and military-related R & D companies, Major Clayton R. Stone, ex-Special Forces, ex-Ranger, ex just about every goddamned thing you could name, had both the resources and the expertise to plan and build the shelter. While other men were building fallout shelters made of concrete tubes sunk a few feet into the earth—the major had the whole inside of a granite slope blasted out, creating tens of thousands of square feet of survival space for his family. Stone had never even gotten along with the son of a bitch that well in life; the two had argued from just about the day he was born. But he had to admit, in the brave new world that was America, he was grateful he had the place to come to now. Without it, he would have been just another dying man in the woods.

He walked up to a large boulder about thirty feet in front of the steep face that rose up more thousands of feet above them capped with white diamond fields of snow. Putting his shoulder against it, he pushed with all his might. It hadn't been that difficult to move the boulder in the past, but then he'd had two legs to work with. Falling on his face several times, Stone at last managed to get the thing rolled over a few feet and reached down into the three-foot-deep hole. He pulled up a small plastic bag. He stood up, took out a small device from the bag, and pointed it at the solid rock wall.

The mountain opened. Two three-foot-thick, ten-foot-high granite sections slid silently apart. Stone lurched forward, his wounded leg throbbing up painfully again as streams of fire coursed through his veins. The dog trotted happily alongside of him. It knew what the cavern built into the side of a mountain contained—food. More food than it had seen for days. And for the dog that was just about tantamount to entering the very doors of paradise. It flopped its tongue out and began salivating up a flood before they had gone three yards inside.

The doors closed automatically behind him and Stone glanced around the outer garage, with its few cars still parked around. Nothing looked disturbed. But he was careful. There had been an infiltration once before. There couldn't be another. Stone pushed open the door that led to the main living quarters, and the dog let out a happy bark as it entered into the warmth and safety of the bunker. The entire place was operated by computer, so although no lights were on, when Stone walked from room to room, they automatically switched on and off around him. His father had set up the place so that it was theoretically self-sufficient for the next twenty years or more. Air and water were purified and recycled. Life-support systems, lighting, temperature, plant watering, all were controlled by a Cray II Super Computer, possibly the only one still operating, as not too many people were using such things in the hellhole that America had become. Except maybe as a latrine.

As Stone headed into the living quarters, the pit bull again rushed all around his feet like a living bolo.

"What the hell are you, dog, a cat?" Stone asked, almost tripping again. "Cats are supposed to slither all around their master's legs, not *dogs*. Now get some canine etiquette in that dumb brain, okay?" The animal just looked up at him with saliva-dripping sincerity and kept rushing back and forth only inches ahead of him banging into the walls. Stone walked through the large communal area that his family— the major, his mother, and sister April, God help their souls —had spent most of the five years they had inhabited the place. His father had known there was going to be war— and he had been right. The night he had a dream warning of the blood fire to follow, he packed the whole family up at two in the morning and they drove from their Denver home here to his little oasis in the middle of nowhere. They had barley arrived when they saw the huge atomic sparks to the north and east. They had gone inside and locked the doors. For five fucking years.

Stone could feel their ghosts. He always could. It was as though they were right there. His sister, playing with her MacIntosh computer by the glowing logs in the fireplace, glowing electric the moment Stone entered the room. There was his mother knitting, her forehead pinched together as she thought about this or that design she was working on. And his father, down in his computer room, that ran the whole place. Doing God knew what—for five years. A great place to visit, but you wouldn't want to live there. Only, Stone had.

Ghosts! They were moving around now. In his fever and increasing delirium, Stone swore he could see their faces— his father all blue from his heart attack, his mother raped and mutilated by bikers only hours after they had left the place. His sister April—he couldn't see her ghost. That meant *she* was still alive. But for how long?

He headed past the plants still blooming, fed by hydro-ponic units, the goldfish off to one side, given food, oxy-genated, every damn thing. The whole world on auto. Stone had a sudden bizarre thought as he wondered whether the fish got lonely. Cared for completely by machine. Not a human hand ever tapping the glass, eyes looking down. It was weird. He took the mutt to the kitchen, knowing it would drive him crazy for the job that lay ahead of him. A task that would be hard enough without some animal barking up a storm and tearing down the place. The dog's hunger on top of the food smells in the kitchen made it go half mad with excitement the moment they walked inside. It leaped up and around in the air in a corkscrewing motion like some kind of dolphin out of water.

"Cool it, garbage barge," Stone said sharply. All he needed was for one of the animal's leaping nips to take off his nose or chin or something that he'd rather keep. He'd seen what the canine's dagger jaws could do. It was like standing next to a spinning propeller. Stone pulled out some cans at random from the well-stocked shelves above. His mother, who liked to cook, had been, in a claustrophobic sort of way, in heaven. With twenty years' worth of supplies, canned food, frozen meats, and vegetables. Everything, even a gourmet chef would have been proud to use. Post—Collapse of Civilization chefs, anyway.

But Stone wasn't serving any flaming horse meat tonight. Wincing with pain as he held up one of the cans to the electric opener, Stone opened tuna fish, then undid a bottle of pickles, then pulled a frozen steak out of one of the freezers and threw it all down in a big Tupperware bowl.

"Now eat slow, big boy," Stone said with a smirk, knowing that was the last thing in the world the animal was likely to do. The dog tore into the feast like a great white shark hitting into a sea lion. Pickle chunks, frozen meat that shattered when the dog clamped into it—all flew off in different directions, splattering the floor and the side of the refrigerator.

"Oh, God," Stone muttered to himself, turning and limping off. Well, the dog would just have to lick up all that it had just centrifuged off—because Stone might not be around for a while. He hobbled back out to the connecting hall and down to the end of it. He keyed in a code on a small inset keyboard and a steel door slid open, allowing him entry. The place never ceased to amaze him. He walked into his father's computer/communications/scientific lab—the thousand square feet of space where he had spent the last five years of his life, never allowing any of them to enter.

Stone hadn't ever seen the inside of the room until after the major's death.

And he had been in for a shock. For among the many things the major had been doing was filling a computer full of information. Everything that he had learned in his long career as a fighting Ranger in four different major wars— and he had lost track of how many minor, secret, unpublicized ones—had been preserved for his son on tape. A way to communicate from the grave, to send Stone information in magnetic form that had already saved his ass.

Stone walked through the beeping, clicking, flashing maze of computers, radar receivers, tapes recording every CB message that came in. This, too, would all go on for decades, or so the major had assured them all. And he had reason to doubt the man's word or foresight. As much as Martin hated to admit it, the old man had turned out to be right about *every* goddamn thing. Stone had inherited a bleak, violent world—along with the firepower and other resources to fight back.

Not that it looked like he was going to be running around too much. In fact, as he swooned and had to catch hold of the chair in front of him he realized with horror that he didn't have any time at all. If he went out, from loss of blood, shock, whatever, he wasn't coming back. And as much as the dog had helped him a number of times, the mutt wasn't a fucking surgeon capable of giving him IV's and making the incisions to remove the festering flesh along one leg. Which meant Stone was going to have to do it.

He sat down in the pneumatic work chair and clicked on the computer terminal. The whole system was designed to be UUF—Ultra User Friendly, meaning he hardly had to know shit about the thing to use it. Stone had already obtained information from it on tank formations when he had been involved in a tank battle months before—and on the location of some missile sites in Utah. Again the Cray had been right. Now he needed info of a different kind. To say the least. Tank formations were nothing compared to . . . operating on himself.

YES? the computer lit up, the words scrolling across the screen.

MEDICAL, Stone typed in on the keyboard. Instantly the screen switched to a list of medical subcategories from diseases to surgery. Stone slammed in the choice and the screen listed more specific types of injuries. Soon he had it narrowed down to about the situation he was in—SURGERY FOR BROKEN LEG WITH POSSIBLE GANGRENE DEVELOPMENT. A three-dimensional representation of a leg appeared on the screen and began turning in several directions at once, giving him different views from every angle. The leg was all charted out with a grid so he could indicate just where the injury was and the approximate direction and extent of the break.

TREATMENT? Stone keyed in.

GANGRENOUS PORTIONS MUST BE REMOVED SURGICALLY, VEINS CAUTERIZED IN AREA. BONE MUST BE RESET USING HYPERBURLIC METAL STRAPPING SYSTEM. SEE STORAGE BIN 87AA. He studied the chart closely as the computer continued to make the 3-D image of the leg move before him as if an invisible hand was twisting it around. A scalpel appeared and showed the exact angle to slice. Then the image of the metal tightening band that was to be put around the leg and tightened by hand was demonstrated. After memorizing all the information, he keyed in another question.

SURGICAL SUPPLIES AVAILABLE?

The screen immediately displayed the location of all the items needed for the operation around the communications room. His father had equipped the place as well with an entire mini medical/operating facility. The more he investigated the room the more it seemed to reveal, like a high-tech onion pulling back layers of function. Stone found the drugs first and, following the computer's advice, gave himself a megavitamin shot, then a superpotent antibiotics mixture. He unlatched a stainless-steel operating table that was hinged to one wall. Most of the supplies were arranged on shelves on the walls on each side of the long stainless-steel table. Within about ten minutes, Stone had everything set up.

It was going to be the craziest piece of surgery mankind had ever performed on itself. And if there was such a thing as the AMA (American Medical Association) anymore, which there wasn't, they would doubtless have sued the living shit out of him. On the other hand, since he was going to do it to himself, if he fucked up there would be no one to sue. Or something like that. His head was getting dizzier.

"Come on, Dr. Kildare," Stone mocked himself, trying to get his courage up. He set the video camera in place so that he could see everything clearly on a TV monitor on a table to the right side about a yard away. He proceeded to cut the whole side of his pants leg to the thigh so the bleeding mess was exposed. It was worse than he had thought. Jesus, it was hard to look at. His own flesh—all purple and fucked up like it was ready for the grave. He wished suddenly he'd taken more time to treat it days before. But he'd been on the run—there had been no time. And now he was running out of said quantity; the last few grains were suspended tremblingly on the edge of the hourglass of Martin Stone's life.

The pain was too much as Stone, sitting up, tried to slice away at the poisoned flesh, just above the knee on the inside of the thigh. The skin was clearly dead, some of it with a brown, even blackish, appearance. He tried to cut into it, but the combined pain of the broken bone plus the slicing was too much. Stone fell backward onto the table, where at least the broken bone seemed to be relieved from the pressure. He reached over for the mechanical hands he had set up. His father had known a man might have to operate on himself. For in the new world, there was not a hospital still operating, not a single soul that one could depend on for anything.

Stone fitted his hands inside the input section of the device, gloves that his fingers could manipulate easily. The futuristic-looking aluminum gloves had wires and gears that fed into a pair of mechanical steel hands attached to long robotic arms that could swivel and turn in any direction. They had been originally developed for radioactive-material handling, but over the years had been used for numerous kinds of technologies. It had been simple enough for his father to obtain an advanced model of the species. Stone tried the gloves, manipulating them a few times as he turned his head to the side and watched on the TV monitor—all in living gory color. He could see the leg just sitting there waiting for more of its blood to flow. He made one of the mechanical hands reach down and take a large cotton cloth from the table and dip it in a bowl of alcohol. Then he moved it up and down the gangrenous area, scraping away all the surface rot. He winced as he moved his hand within the glove. The pain was amazing, even though he thought he was prepared for it.

With the top layers of rot gone, he pushed the close-up button on the wireless video transmitter that sat next to him on the operating table. The camera zoomed in, and he could see now that maybe it wasn't as bad as he had thought. The actual dead tissue was about as big as a silver dollar; the rest was bruised badly, but still seemed to be on the side of the living. Stone made the mechanical hand lift a scalpel and, letting out a long breath, he dug in. He screamed. And screamed again. But never took his eyes from the video monitor—or allowed himself to pass out. Painkilling drugs were out of the question, as they would dull his manual dexterity and hand-eye coordination, which were vital if there was any chance of success.

After about ten seconds of cutting here and there, he could see that he had excised all of the black muck. He cut around the edges once more. And again let out a long howl like a stuck dog. And for a second he thought he heard Excaliber answering far off from the kitchen. When he finished cutting and once again examined the area, he took a large cotton swab, had the mechanical hand dip it in hydrogen peroxide, and painted the whole area. It stung like a motherfucker. Then he smeared antibiotic salves over the whole thing and placed a thick piece of gauze down on it covered over with tape.

That was the *easy* part. Now was the hard. Gripping the

HyperBurlic steel leg band with both mechanical hands, he opened it up and put it beneath the broken part of the thigh. Pulling the two pieces of steel band around, he attached them in groves so they locked together. Looking in the monitor, he moved the mechanical hand to the top of the band, where a handle turned a screw gear. He turned it. And the pain was a tidal wave that swept over his entire soul. But he turned and kept on turning, looking through teary eyes at the screen, making sure he was putting the pressure in the right place so the broken bone would set into proper alignment. Still, he had to do a bunch of yelling to get the thing tightened the full three turns that the computer had dictated.

When it was all done and he lay there breathing hard, Stone allowed himself to rest. The operation was complete. The rest was up to God. And as he started to try to rise up to head to the bedroom, it was as if all his energy suddenly drained down into the operating table he was lying on. And he fell into a pit that was red and had jagged cutting edges.

FOUR

When he awoke he was still lying on the operating table—in a pool of his own blood. He snapped open his stuck eyes in horror, thinking perhaps he was near bleeding to death. But as he sat up, Stone saw that it was all from the operation. He looked down at the leg. The part he had sliced out throbbed like a war drum, but the bandage around it, although stained with an initial flow of blood, was not wet now. He had succeeded—momentarily. Whether or not he had terminated the gangrene threat he'd find out soon enough. The band of steel that was tightened around the break had pretty much numbed out the whole area with the pressure it was putting on. The computer had said the band should stay on for forty-eight hours so the bones could begin knitting properly —then be followed by a cast. Right! He'd just check into the local emergency room.

Stone swung his legs over the side of the table and stepped down gingerly onto the floor. Not too bad. He could even put a little weight on the broken leg, though it didn't feel great. He grabbed a crutch from the wall and walked around testing it as the banks of computers beeped out pulsing streams of information around him. He cleaned up the operating area a little, at least getting rid of the bloody rags, and then headed out down toward the living quarters.

He gasped as he rounded the bend and looked into the kitchen. The pit bull's food had long since vanished, but it looked as though the dog had helped itself to more. A lot more. The mutt had somehow learned to open the cabinets above the sinks where the cans and what all were stored. And had pulled down a large number of them, which lay bitten up around the floor. The dog was nowhere in sight.

"Son of a bitch," Stone muttered, walking along on the crutch as little waves of pain shot up the leg. At least he didn't feel as feverish. That was a good sign. He hit the living quarters and glanced around, still not seeing a sign of the animal, though the place looked as if a tornado had gone through it. Whether the animal had had a bad stomach after all the feasting, or had just been exuberant and wanted a night on the town, Stone didn't know. And it didn't really matter what its motivation, just the results. The couches were on their sides, pillows all over the place. The two large rugs—one Persian, the other plush white fur—had been chewed and rolled around so that dog hair coated their surfaces like a sprinkling of volcanic ash.

Stone saw a motion from beneath an upturned armchair and angrily hobbled over. He kicked the chair aside and there, bloated as a bloodworm, with bloodshot eyes and hangdog expression of the highest order, Excaliber stared back at him. Its stomach hung way out on the front side of it as if the damn thing had swallowed a boulder.

"What the hell do you have to say for yourself, dog?" Stone hissed with barely repressed rage. The dog just whined a little sound, as though it could hardly get up the strength to even do that. Its hanging eyes seemed to be begging for Alka-Seltzer or some damn thing that would ease it out of its culinary hangover. Twenty pounds of food crammed into a ninety-pound frame was not exactly the way to feel good the next morning. Stone walked around, turning things upright, kicking the coffee table back in place. His mother's ghost hovered over the place commanding him to tidy up. She would be having a shit fit, Stone thought darkly, if she were here now. When they had lived together she would scold him for leaving a book out on a couch. The dog had sent the slowly deteriorating scene in the bunker right over the edge.

But whatever thoughts Stone had about getting the place in at least less chaotic form were suddenly interrupted by a beeping sound that came blasting over the bunker's PA.

"EMERGENCY   TRANSMISSION,   EMERGENCY TRANSMISSION. COME TO COMPUTER ROOM. EMERGENCY TRANSMISSION." Stone muttered a few choice curses under his breath, wondering if he was ever going to get even a second's rest, and dropped the pillow he was lifting back down, where it settled with a little rush of feathers where the dog had chewed some good-size holes, apparently hallucinating that the thing was a chicken during the course of its food nightmares.

He headed back down to the communications room and slammed himself down in one of the seats in front of the console that was screaming out all kinds of emergency signals. Stone pressed the Play button and sat back. His father's equipment constantly monitored all frequencies, searching for CB, radio—anything it could find. Which wasn't a hell of a lot. It was also coded through the computer, to immediately pick up on key words. Martin Stone was one of them. And Stone could see immediately why it had sent out the alert.

"Martin Stone, Stone, come in," a voice was saying over the loudspeaker on the wall. "This is La Junta calling Martin Stone. We have your sister, Stone. Do you hear? She is our prisoner. We are willing to talk terms. Come to La Junta. Calling Stone, Martin Stone." That was it, just repeated over and over as if it was on a tape loop. It didn't tell him a hell of a lot. But it told him enough. His sister was once again hanging to this life by her fingernails.

FIVE

They danced naked in the moonlight. The full moon that beat down on them like an illuminating fire of passion and madness. Women, dozens of them, undulated and writhed like the legions of the possessed. Their bodies were covered with sweat as they danced around a large cleared field, their firm breasts swinging and rising and falling as they spun and leaped into the air to unheard music. The moonlight was strong, brilliant as it poured down over their weaving bodies, bathing them in its magic light. For countless centuries folk tales had spoken of the Moon Madness, the hypnotic trance into which people fell, under its spell—the strange things they might do.

Though the women danced in the moonlight in rigorous pulsations, their faces were without joy or pleasure of the slightest kind. Their faces were dead, frozen. More like the features of stone than the living, the desiring. The contrast was strange between the wild gyrations and the flat expressions. Not that one of them had the consciousness to notice such things. For they were without thought. Were only what the Guru told them. He was their mentor, their leader, their god. And he played with them like puppets, his own personal playthings that he could do with as he wished.

Guru Yasgar stood on a crude platform made of branches

at one side of the field and exhorted them on. He wore a full black robe and raised his hands high, as if commanding the moon itself. He was all. He was the great one. To be feared, to be obeyed at once. To give one's life for. As many had.

Guru Yasgar waved his hand to the right and some servants came forward holding large gourds of a golden-hot nectar. The women stopped only long enough to drink huge slugs of the stuff—five, six gulps until it was running down their chins, down their golden bodies. Then they rejoined the dancing, tossing their heads from side to side as they flew wildly about. They were like wild animals, and as the night grew deeper the Guru screamed out magic incantations, spinning his arms in the air. The women grew even more frenzied and clawed at each other and themselves in a rising madness. They bit and punched as they danced, all trying to leap higher than the others, as if trying to grab the very moon from the sky and make love to it. For their eyes were filled with an unquenchable desire, their lips parted, begging for release, release. But Yasgar only played with them. He was the cat—and they were his mice.

"Faster! Faster!" Yasgar commanded. For the frenzy was not wild enough, the blood not flowing freely enough to satisfy his cravings, his bloodlust. He pulled a horsewhip from within his robe and snapped it into the air above their heads so that it made a thunderous crack.

"Dance, you bitches, dance!" Yasgar screamed, his black rat eyes as dark as pits within the fat jowled face, the whip cracking out again and again, ever closer to their soft spinning flesh. Now they moved faster. Fear was the great motivator. Fear was what made the world go round. What made empires rise—and fall.

Guru Yasgar's little empire had begun when he was just a kid. A snot-nosed six-year-old who saw that his mental powers, his will, were stronger than the other children's. It was an easy thing to intimidate them, make them give him their lunches, change, even books and sweaters. He rarely had to fight to back up his aggressiveness. But when he did, those who challenged him wished they hadn't. For the child was like a wild beast when he grew angry—biting, spitting, using any weapon at hand. And he would hurt them. Bones would be broken, eyes would come free from their sockets, teeth from their fleshy grooves.

As the child grew older and entered puberty, he discovered that his willpower worked just as well over the opposite sex, too. In no time he had a little harem going and was pimping to the other high school kids. His girls brought him *all* the money—for already his wrath was something not to be brought down on oneself. By the age of fifteen, he had killed one of them. She had made the mistake of stealing from him. Her body was found floating in a nearby river a few months later. Her head was never recovered.

The young Yasgar's greatest idol during these formative years was Charles Manson. The way Manson had used his own willpower and the manipulation of sex was like a Red Sea Scroll for the criminally evolving teen. And once he discovered that he could get control over groups of men as well—by using the girls to seduce them, by having orgies that he directed, as Manson had done—the world was his. The great director—of human lives. A role he found most pleasing. By the age of twenty, he had an arrest sheet five yards long. But the longest the cops could ever put him away for was six months. And even then he got out in two for good behavior. Which he set up by having two of his fifteen-year-old "virgins" sleep with the warden. It was pitiful how easy it was to ascend in this world of weak minds and even weaker flesh.

But the law was closing in on him on the East Coast, to which up until now he had confined his operations. So becoming Guru Yasgar, he moved out to Colorado, where he knew there were a number of cults, communes, off in the hills. The perfect place to let his brand of cancer breed. He bought nearly a thousand acres in the southeastern part of the state, below La Junta. Starting out with an initial two dozen or so followers, within five years Yasgar had hundreds. And having virtual slave labor, he had been able to build—a city. A minicity of rough-hewn wood cabins and a three-story palace, a bizarre oriental-looking monstrosity of Guru Yasgar's own twisted design.

It wasn't hard to attract more and more followers. Men and women crave sex. Society so represses the animal urges and instincts, male and female are so embattled and pushed apart, that Yasgar could manipulate it all to his own dark ends. The orgies grew ever larger, until it was as if Yasgar were directing an epic rather than something of human scale. Yet still he wasn't satisfied, still wanted to make his "cleansing" process, which basically brainwashed his new recruits into the ways of his cult—the Perfect Aura—faster, more efficient. Wanted his control to be total and absolute. Wanted *their* submission to be a hundred percent.

He began experimenting with drugs—mixtures of heroin, cocaine, Demerol, pentothal, and other mind-altering concoctions. Drugs used on schizophrenics, on horses, on elephants. And though some died in his attempts to create just the right mixture, at last success was his. With this Golden Elixir—and the super speeded up brain-"cleansing" techniques he had developed over the years—Yasgar could take a man or woman and bring them from the outside to total slavehood within three days. He challenged any other guru or warlord to meet that demanding statistic. Not that there were any newsletters so they could all exchange brain recipes. But he knew his power. He proved it every minute of every day. And that was what mattered. That a living god be worshipped by more and more of humanity. Numbers mattered. Perhaps someday the entire world would be his.

Yasgar looked down at them, at the beauteous flesh twisting around, every part of their bodies moving in a different direction as if they were quicksilver, were streams of rain. He looked at their nubile flesh, their perfect breasts. And began choosing which ones he would have tonight, would play with back in his "palace."

"Dance," he screamed out in commanding deep tones, like the very voice of a living god. "Dance or die," he chanted, cracking out the long bullwhip, which danced above their heads like a wind-blown tendril beneath the ghost moon, whipping ever closer, taking little bites out of thighs and breasts, cheeks, shoulders, buttocks. He was maddened with sick desire now, beneath the robe. He felt flushed with the supreme control of the women, their flesh broken and bleeding beneath his hands. It was the highest of pleasures that a dark god could feel on this earth.

SIX

Stone had just one problem—aside from a broken leg that might or might not have to be amputated and a fever of a 102 that wouldn't break. He'd lost all his firepower and his Harley 1200cc bike when he'd been caught in an avalanche and swept right off the side of a mountain. He wasn't about to venture out into the wilds without a miniwarwagon. But that meant building one up—almost from scratch. In spite of the pain that kept streaming up and down the leg, he headed out to the garage to see just what the hell was there to work with.

A quick perusal of the three cars, two motorcycle frames and assorted spare wheels, engines, and transmissions showed him that it was possible. It was going to be a pretty ugly-looking hybrid, that was for damn sure. Stone dragged a motorcycle frame on a dolly over to a hydraulic work station. Attaching the frame to various bolts and clamps, he pressed a button on the lift's side and it rose a yard off the ground, making the frame easily accessible from every side. Stone got out the welding equipment from the corner, an oxy/acetylene job. His father had made sure that there were extras of everything, so that if one vehicle went, they could strip the others. It meant that from a total of three cars and several bike frames, they could end up with five or six vehicles over a number of years—progressively uglier, no doubt, but there weren't too many beauty contests these days. He attached a chain to the engine, a Harley 1400cc, a little higher-powered than his old bike but not any larger in cubic feet. It was a slightly more advanced model that the major had picked up just months before the whole ball game collapsed. It would soup the bike up to higher acceleration and cruising speeds, though already he'd been near the limit of his ability to hang on half the time. A more powerful bike was a little hard to imagine.

He moved the mobile chain pulley and set the engine inside the bike and he quickly began welding it to the frame. Stone thanked God now that he had spent three summers working in Sprague's Auto Repair Shop. By the time he'd left to go to college, he was one of the best mechanics in the place. Al himself had offered Stone a job starting at $250 per week. Not bad for a teenager. Now there were hardly enough operating cars left in America to employ a full garage of mechanics. Times had changed. When these were gone, there wouldn't be any more.

Stone had to grab a visored mask and throw it over his head as the sparks began flying all around him in showers of white. He felt dizzy from the fever. But the work, the movement, also got blood rushing through his veins, blood with healing antibodies to fight infection, with fresh bone marrow to begin building new linkages of bone within his fractured leg. It felt good—just to be alive after what he'd been through recently. Stone got the engine welded in place, then the transmission, all within three hours. In another two, the seats, the weapons clamps—everything else—was in place as well.

Stone stood back and surveyed what he had wrought. It looked like a child that shouldn't have been born. Like five different bikes squeezed into one, which was just about the case. The wheels seemed a little too big, too wide, more like they should be on a car. The seat was a good foot longer than his old one, as though it belonged to a bike twice as large. The bars pulled up into the air semibiker style. All in all, it was a mechanical mutation that Evel Knievel would undoubtedly have been proud of. Now all Stone had to do was give it some teeth.

He stopped off in the kitchen to get some coffee, and saw that the dog was at it again. It was hard for Stone to believe it could want more, with its stomach already so swollen that it looked as if it had a huge cancerous tumor dragging all the way down to the ground. But the dog was scrounging around the huge mess of rotting food that it had created the night before, and sniffing as if it had pretensions to gourmethood. Every few seconds it leaned down and picked up a choice item—pickled pear, chunk of spam, syrup-coated peach squirming around the floor like a rogue eyeball. Stone avoided the mess completely, not even vaguely able to deal with cleaning it all up. Maybe if he just let the mutt lick away for a few more hours there wouldn't be anything left to clean.

He made himself a whole Thermos full of coffee and, sipping slowly, as it nearly scalded his lips, he headed down the hall to the weapons room to see what he was going to turn a vehicle into a warwagon with. His father had been no slouch in the armaments department either. But then, being the president of a multinational munitions company didn't hurt matters any. There was wall-to-wall, floor-to-ceiling steel shelving covered with crates filled with handguns and rifles, ammunition . . . and the bigger stuff as well. Mortars, tripod-mounted .50 caliber machine guns that could pierce armor. And even bigger stuff than that—handheld rocket launchers, the Luchaire 89mm missile system that Stone had used previously, and had found to be very effective, to say the least. He took it down from the shelf. The last one; after this there were no more. He put it in an industrial cart with wheels and pushed the cart on around the square room, which contained an amazing amount of firepower, considering. Stone was trying to walk without the crutch already. It hurt like he was being tortured—but with the steel band tightly around the broken area, it seemed to at least hold the whole thing together. He knew he was doing wonders for his body and would be a complete wreck by the time he hit fifty. On the other hand, since he probably wouldn't live past thirty, he wasn't going to start worrying about it.

Next he took a small crate of rockets—a half-dozen of them, then a .50-caliber machine gun, with automatic belt feed. Stone walked on around the shelves, which towered up above him filled to overflow with the products of the dark side of man's technological expertise. But if the other bastards had them, Stone wanted them too. And worse. He reached up and took down a sawed-off Browning 12-gauge autofire shotgun. That would do nicely—and a hundred rounds of ammo. Then, for personal use, a Beretta PM 12S, stripped-down version, 9mm, and with twenty-, thirty-, even fifty-round clips that could be fired singly or on full auto, emptying a whole load in seconds. And finally—for his takeout handgun—another Ruger Red Hawk .44 with twelve-inch barrel. The thing would have made Clint Eastwood green with envy. He strapped it on. It made Stone feel very secure.

He pushed the shopping cart of destruction out of the room and back down the hall. He was walking into the lion's den. How did the poem go? "Do not go gentle into that good night." Well, it wasn't a good night—it was a rotting, screaming night. And he wasn't going gentle, but kicking, blasting his resistance to the last second. Back in the garage, Stone used the block and tackle to haul up the machine gun first. He set it down right between the raised handlebars like a water buffalo's horns, and getting the right-size steel clamps to hold it in place, welded it down. He tested it, turning the wheel back and forth. The machine gun was set as if in concrete. Then the Luchaire missile tube—about three feet long, twelve inches wide—to the side of the bike.

It was slow going, making sure the ball-bearing hinges were angled just right. For even a slight angle off made the tube scrape against the bike when he opened it out. But at last, with a little more fiddling with the welding torch, Stone had that set in too. Then the rack for the shells right below it so he could pop one out from the top of the spring-loaded container tube by just pushing a release button. It gave him the ability to load and fire the 89mm rocket within five seconds.

Finally Stone took some steel boxes from one of the shelves of the garage and mounted them as well on the back of the bike. Storage for ammunition, tent, med supplies, and spare clothes. After spending nearly the whole day on the project, he stood back and looked. It was definitely one of the weirder gasoline vehicles ever to roll along the planet earth. Even the dog, when he came snooping around from its floor mopping, made a sucked-in face and let out a howl of derision, like "You expect me to ride on that hunk of shit?"

But when Stone lowered the completely assembled motorcycle back down to the ground and sat atop the thing trying it out—testing the feel of the bars, the give of the seat—the pit bull jumped on behind him and began sniffing around, snarling and biting at the thick leather as if he wasn't sure if it was enemy or friend.

SEVEN

With the bike assembled, Stone headed to the kitchen to see what the dog had wrought. It had licked clean the entire floor. The animal was a junkie, an addict of anything that didn't make him puke. And he had eaten a few of those in his day as well.

"It's diet time again, pal," Stone said with a disgusted look at the canine, which stood in the doorway looking up as if he'd had nothing to do with the mess. Stone grabbed a mop from the closet and slopped it around the floor. "And don't look at me with those pathetic puppy-dog eyes, 'cause you ain't been a puppy for eons now, and the eyes have gotten a little bloodshot around the edges. You'd better start thinking of shipping out to the Betty Ford Clinic for some mental and physical rehabilitation." But the fighting canine just snorted, not wanting to hear any bull this hungry morning. It took Stone nearly half an hour to get the place in a vague kind of order, and that was just getting the stickiest of the puddles off the floor, wiping the splattered bits of food from the china closet and the refrigerator, the rows of shelves. The animal believed in the tornado approach to eating—swallow everything and spit out what you don't like.

An hour later, Stone was on the bike and heading out into the hard world. He stopped the Harley by the boulder where the transmitter was kept hidden, and stood up. It was hard going, what with the steel clamp around his thigh and the huge bandage taped around the incised section. But already he was getting used to dealing with the thing and swung the whole leg smoothly up over the seat. The dog didn't move an inch, just clamped onto the black leather, eyes peering from beneath its paws.

Stone was pleased to see that the bike stayed upright on the wide footrest he had welded on. He still wasn't quite sure everything was going to hold up. He pushed the boulder back from the hole and, wrapping the door opener up in its plastic bag, placed it carefully down inside. Then he rolled the boulder back over the top. He never knew each time he left the bunker whether or not he would ever see it again. And this time it seemed even more unlikely than the previous departures. The sky was growing dark overhead, even though it wasn't midday yet. The air was sharp with an icy blade that bit into his eyes and skin. The steel clamp around his leg was already burning with cold. Things were just great. Stone got back on the Harley, kicked it into gear, and headed into hell.

He was nervous for the first few minutes, taking the homemade vehicle slow along the narrow deer paths that led back down the side of the slope. If he went over now in the state he was in, he might not be getting back up again. But to Stone's pleasure, on a day that was about as hospitable as the inside of a coffin, at least the bike seemed to be functioning perfectly. The Harley 1400cc seemed to have a lot more acceleration than the old bike. It was slightly heavier, though if anything that gave it a lower center of gravity, setting it down on its wide tires like a small tank. The only thing a little disconcerting were the different-shaped handlebars, which were more upright and swept back than his old ones. But after about half an hour of getting used to the new cycle, Stone began getting used to the bars as well—and found that if he just lay back in the ol' saddle the bike almost steered itself.

He reached the end of the hidden access road to the

bunker and moved at a crawl through the thicket of brambles and vines that formed a camouflage ahead. There was a good thirty feet of the stuff, and the dog let out with a few sharp howls as its hide was pricked by brambles. Then they were through, and Stone looked around behind him to make sure that from the single-lane country road he was now on, you couldn't see that there was anything heading off into the mountains. The bunker had been built in just about the most inaccessible place in these parts. Stone shuddered to think what could happen if some psycho got hold of the bunker— its weapons and supplies.

He headed south down the one-laner, which quickly turned to two. The road was already an obstacle course of cracks and potholes. It hadn't taken long for civilization's trappings to begin crumbling. Still, Stone was able to open up his handiwork a little when he hit a straightaway. And the son of a bitch nearly took off. Within seconds he was going seventy, then eighty, then ninety miles per hour. The dog let out a strange sound from the back, and as Stone saw that the road got much rougher just ahead he slammed on the brakes, figuring it was as good a time as any to test them. They were too good. Being used to the looser brakes of the 1200, Stone pulled hard. The wheels locked and the bike just skidded along, stirring up a cloud of leaves and dust behind him.

It was only his skill and fast reflexes that kept the Harley upright, though the pit bull came unlodged from its clamped hold and crashed into Stone's back in a flurry of paws and angry barks. Then he had the cycle under control again and slowed it down to twenty as he headed over some potholes that you could have buried a cow in. But at last everything was back to more or less normal and the two of them dug in for the long haul. As Stone hit more good patches of road, he eased the bike up to the forty, then fifty, range. The wide tires made going over the rough road a little easier than the old bike would have done. All in all, not a bad trade-in.

They rode through the late afternoon, the dog standing up on its hind quarters, once it had gotten used to the feel of the new machine, with its front paws up over Stone's shoulder so the human and the furred head were fully focused on the world ahead of them. The two-laner went on for about twenty miles, then changed to an interstate. Stone had used part of it before. Some sections were still as good as the day they had been built, others as if they had been through a hurricane. Still, it was worth using it, considering the time it would buy him on the good stretches. The first ten miles or so was easy going, and it was almost possible to imagine that he was in the pre-Collapse days, heading out for a little spin in the country with the family dog. Yeah, right—armed with a .50-caliber up front and so much firepower strapped to the bike and inside of his jacket that he could have taken on Napoleon at Waterloo.

They came to what had been an old tollbooth collection junction, with wide curving ramps joing the interstate from several directions. Stone slowed the Harley to a crawl and eased it through the opening between two of the six toll stations through which thousands of cars had once rolled. He felt a bizarre twinge of guilt as he rolled through without paying his money, the rusted bucket reaching for some change. Almost immediately on the far side of the toll plaza he began to drive past rusting carcasses of cars, on the sides of the road and on the highway itself. It quickly became an obstacle course to get through. Within ten minutes it was so inundated with rusting bodies, as if the heavens had rained automobiles, that Stone had to drop the bike down to a walk so that he could balance it with both feet down on each side.

Brown twisted frames, with wheels and glass long gone. Inside some were still the original occupants—now just skeletons, lying on their seats, sitting as if in an eternal traffic jam from which they would never emerge. It felt a little spooky to pass a car, look in its paneless window, and see a skull smiling back at you. He didn't stop to chat.

The car graveyard lasted for nearly twenty miles. A hell of a lot of people must have been caught in the blast of a nuke or something, Stone mused, for so many to have been taken out like this at once. Then, as he went around a curve and over a rise, they disappeared again. Stone quickly built up to thirty, then forty, as the interstate got hillier and began undulating up and down like a snake so that he started feeling dizzy and heard the dog burping behind him as if it might lose some of the vast feast that was still squeezing through its clogged digestive system.

As he started down the next hill, Stone saw a roadblock ahead. A wide barricade of wood and car hulks, cinder blocks—you name it, it was in his way. Everything, including literally a few kitchen sinks. He had to slam on the brakes hard, as the blockade was only about seventy yards down the hill. The bike came to rest about thirty feet from the wall of junk. Stone put his hand up on the trigger of the .50-caliber as he saw shapes running behind the eight-foot-or-so-high barricade of all the debris that would make a trashman ecstatic.

Suddenly Stone saw figures jumping down from the barrier, and coming out from around the sides. There were dozens of them—and every ugly son-of-a-bitching one of them was wearing a baseball uniform, a cap, and carrying a bat. If they were a baseball team they looked like they'd been playing with human heads, for their uniforms were splattered in blood, torn and tattered as if a few knives and bullets had gone through them. And the bats that they held menacingly in their hands looked a little worse for wear, with long cracks, splinters along their sides—and coated red from handle to head. Stone was glad he hadn't seen any of the "games."

"Hold it right there, mister," a huge fat lug of a fellow bellowed out from atop the pile of debris. He held a long bat in one hand and slapped it into the palm of the other as though he was just looking for something or someone he could pound into a pulp, into pâté for the evening's appetizer. "What team you play for?" the man asked, pulling his filthy cap, an old Yankee one if Stone's eyes weren't failing him, up from his eyes.

"Free agent," Stone smirked back. "Don't play for no team, just trying to get through here."

"No one gets through here—unless they answer the riddle," the man shouted. Suddenly he jumped all the way down from the top, a good eight feet, and landed with a thud on the cement highway that they had effectively sealed off from passage.

"And what riddle is that?" Stone asked, letting his finger edge even closer to the trigger of the .50-caliber.

"Who won the American League batting championship in 1977?" the man asked with a dark look. Stone hadn't the slightest idea.

"Daffy Duck," he snorted back as the pit bull whined behind him, edging its furred head around his shoulder to see what was causing the delay in travel arrangements.

"Wrong, asshole," the blood-splattered Yankee-uniformed leader of the gang spat back with a smile on his face, since he knew they were about to end up with one mean-looking motorcycle and a whole shitload of weapons. None who had been unfortunate enough to pass this way had left. "Now, you can just get off that there motorcycle and walk away quick, and I'll let you live," the man lied, "as sure as my name is Squid Ruth, the Babe's grandson himself." Since the asshole's eyes were twitching around in his boil-ridden face, and foam was collecting at the corners of his mouth as he edged forward slapping the bat harder and harder, Stone somehow doubted they were going to let him walk away. And when he saw the streams of Yankee-outfitted bandits coming around each side of the barricade, every one of them swinging a bat, Stone saw that it was time to start doing some hitting of his own.

"Down, dog!" he screamed, praying that the overmacho mutt wouldn't jump off. On the ground the two of them would be dead. That's why Stone had built himself a war-wagon. He just prayed that the sucker worked. As the headman suddenly came charging straight in on him, Stone squeezed hard on the trigger. The .50-caliber snorted out a mouthful of finger-size slugs that dissected the whole front of Ruth's grandson as if he was a pig in a butchering yard. The rib cage exploded out like lathing in a wrecked building and the heart and lungs followed close behind as if they didn't want to be the last ones to desert the sinking ship. The corpse rocketed backward, slamming into the garbage barricade, and slid to the roadway, joining the trash.

The rest of the Yankee team stopped in their tracks as if caught in a rundown play between first and second bases, their bats raised in their trembling arms. Their leader was dead. He had run the team, as general manager and top hitter, for years. The Babe was dead; long live the Babe. And even as they hesitated, trying to regroup, Stone turned the handlebars hard and twisted back on the accelerator. The bike squealed around on a dime, slamming into one of them who had stopped just a few feet away, sending him flying into another little bunch, which toppled over. Stone leaned forward, hoping the dog was making himself scarce on the seat as bats came whizzing in from all over the fucking place. He suddenly knew how a hardball felt as it came in over the batter's box.

But the bike shot through the crowds, and within a few seconds he was beyond their reach. He flew back up the hill he had just traveled down and went a quarter-mile or so to the top before coming to a skidding stop and again twisting the bike around in a one-eighty. The Yankees had stopped and now looked at him from a thousand or so feet away. Stone knew he had plenty of time. Setting the kickstand down, he stepped off the bike and unlatched the Luchaire 89mm. He popped the top shell up from its autofeed and slammed it into the firing tube alongside the bike. He had built this one so it could be fired while he was riding, unlike the previous model, which he had to stop and aim for. Making sure the Luchaire was sighted straight ahead, he remounted and started the bike forward again.

"Hold your ears, dog," Stone said as they started down the hill toward the barricade and the psycho Mickey Mantles who were waiting. The startled heads of the team of killers turned in unison. They weren't expecting this. Nor were they expecting the sudden roar that erupted from Stone's bike as he pulled the trigger on the rocket system. A tail of red and yellow erupted just behind the bike as the missile burst forward in blurred acceleration. It took less than a second for the high-explosive shell to hit into the obstacle a hundred feet ahead.

There was a huge roar and a cloud of smoke rushing everywhere as bodies and tires, sinks and logs, chairs and broken TVs went flying off as though a cyclone had just swept through a garbage dump. Stone didn't wait to see the total results of his little urban-renewal project. He slammed his finger down on the .50-caliber, spraying out a scythe of death in front of him—and tore forward through the smoke, aiming right for where the blast was still rising. Bodies seemed to be everywhere. Stone didn't know if they were after him or just reeling back from the explosion. And he didn't wait to ask. The Harley ripped through them—and then through the blast-created opening in the barricade.

It wasn't a clean opening; the bike shimmied and shook around as the wheels caught on pieces of flaming debris. But it was room enough. For suddenly, with junk being thrown up behind him by the churning paddlewheels of the Harley, he was through. The bike suddenly shot out the other side as if it was flying from a cannon, and Stone was a hundred yards down the highway before he slowed a little and twisted his head around to see what God and his Luchaire had wrought.

It was a mess. He had not just blasted a ten-foot-wide hole through the manmade Maginot Line, but had set the whole thing on fire as well. It burned along a hundred-foot-long stretch and the fingers of flame were moving fast. Atop the barrier, burning men screamed and ran this way and that trapped in a world of pain. Well, the road would be opened up from now on. That was for damn sure, Stone thought darkly. In the game of life and death, it was only *one* strike and you were out.

EIGHT

Stone's heart didn't slow down to something approaching normal for a good three hours and a hundred and fifty miles. Being attacked by psychotic sports teams was something new even for Stone, who thought he had seen just about everything by now. But that was far from the case, he saw as he came around a curve on the interstate and viewed a sight to freeze any man's eyeballs. Two immense H-bomb craters were set about a mile apart. They were gargantuan, towering up into the skies like some sort of mythical creations; the land around them was relatively flat. They were a half-mile in diameter, and their circular craters rose up a good thousand feet before cresting out to a twenty-foot-wide ridge and then sloping back down inside again. Monuments that would survive long after the men who had created them were dust in the ground. Mountains to madness. Towers marking the fatal flaw of man—his genius at creating death.

Stone eased down on the throttle. The craters stood on each side of the interstate, their very lower edges almost touching the side of the road, coming to within yards. Stone wasn't sure just how close he wanted to allow himself to get to these atomic anthills. He had no way of knowing how radioactive they were or weren't. But as he drew closer to the twin craters, Stone's nervousness about proceeding in-

creased with every yard the bike rolled forward. Both
craters, he could see now as the sun was falling from the sky
and bluish darkness was setting in above, were glowing.
One was a bluish color, the other green, as if they had been
hit by different types of bombs or radiation. Stone's eyes
grew wide as he turtled on ahead, for the craters were different in another way as well. The right-hand crater was dead,
black as the dark side of the moon, pockmarked and covered
with a volcanic ash. But the other was . . . alive . . . or something. It was the "or something" that Stone didn't like. For
every second that he drew closer, he could see what looked
like numerous wriggling and slithering things nearly covering the whole slope of the skyscraping crater.

He stopped the bike and took out his field binoculars
from a box behind him as Excalibur snorted nervously on the
seat. The pit bull kept sniffing at the wind, taking deep
breaths and then making a strange expression. Something
was up. God knew what it was. Once Stone got the crater,
only about a quarter-mile off, in focus, he felt like vomiting.
For the undulating worms that covered the whole side of the
bomb crater were like nothing he had seen in his life. And
he wished he hadn't seen these. They didn't look like they
belonged on this earth. They ranged from two to five feet
long, about a foot in diameter, and were covered with spikes
and quills and all kinds of ugly stabbing things. Stone didn't
know if they were animal, vegetable, or a combination of
both. The tubular things seemed more or less anchored to the
ground. But they sure as hell could bend all over the place,
reaching out with long grasping snouts that appeared—
though he couldn't see clearly in the twilight—to have rows
of teeth that hooked backward like sharks'. They kept vacu-
uming down along the ground around them all over the
crater. Stone could barely see some little creatures moving
down below along the slope, though what in God's name
could be up there he didn't think he wanted to meet either.

Suddenly one of the tubes that he happened to be focused
on caught something and lifted it up, holding its prey in its
spiked snout. Just before it chewed down hard, Stone got a

good look at its catch. It looked something like a frog, a frog that was bloodred and had two reptilian heads and long hooked claws instead of webbed feet, and numerous other revolting features. But even as Stone watched, the thing exploded into blood and mush as the tubular plant thing bit down. It swallowed down the twitching creature, all five pounds of it, in two quick bites. Stone could see the shape of the minimonster wriggling within even as it slid down the tubular stem and into the digestive fluids at the base of the thing.

Carnivorous plants. Stone had read about them. Even seen pictures of them in books. But none of them had looked like these. There had never been anything like these before, he was sure of that. Doubtless a scientist would have been ecstatic to witness the disgusting scene. And would have won the Nobel Prize, if there were such things anymore. But Stone was just disgusted, nauseated to the core of his soul. They were alien. Not meant for life here.

Stone had no choice. It was either go down the interstate, which slid right between the two giants, or waste many hours going all the way around the wastelands behind them. And for all he knew, it could be worse out there.

"Okay, dog, pull down your radioactive-proof eye flaps or whatever the hell you've got, 'cause we're going through some hot roadway." Stone wrapped a scarf around his mouth and zippered up the black motorcycle jacket he had taken from the bunker. He eased the bike down the road—and saw with growing horror that the living crater was absolutely covered with the tubular worm things. And every ugly one of them was turning toward Stone and the bike like little radar domes, searching out just what the intruder was—and whether it was edible.

They were even uglier up close. Much, much uglier. For they were the color of blood, with veins running all over them, extending right down into the glowing black soil. They were rooted into the very radioactive crust of the crater. Yet somehow it had given them life, nurtured them, made them grow with wild abandon. They were constantly

moving, twisting, reaching around with their damned eyeless, overtoothed tubes snapping out at anything that came
close—sometimes each other. Then snapping their jaws shut
with reflexive action and biting and chewing at whatever
was there.

And he saw even more little things as he came right between the two craters. Other little mutant creatures rushing
between the roots of the meateaters. They looked as nasty as
the tubes—armored, covered with scales, horns, and bands
of orange and red color that told all the world they were
poisonous as shit to bite into. The whole fucking slope was
alive with the ugly, the diseased, the mutated. Stone prayed
with all he had inside that this wasn't where the new world
was heading. That it wasn't him and his kind that were ob-
solete. That this one mountain was an aberration, a fluke
that would die out and would never be repeated elsewhere.

But if it was dying out, it sure as hell seemed healthy
enough around here. The tubes, some of them ten, even
twelve feet long, snapped out at the bike, which passed just
inches from their reach. One of them stretched out and almost nicked Stone. Excaliber's jaws flew up in a snap, and
with a single bite he severed the head of the thing, churning
jaws and all, and spat it out leaving the headless tube jerking
around in the dust. They had almost gotten clear of the
reaching jungle of teeth when Stone heard a roar off to the
side. The sound was something between what a lion might
emit on a horny jungle night and the trumpet a rogue elephant makes telling all the world to watch out.

Then Stone saw it, and he knew why the beast was so
arrogant. It was the mutant to end mutants. The creature
stood ahead of them in the road, directly in their way.
Stone's jaw hung open in amazement as he stared at the
thing. It was big. At least three or four times as big as Excaliber, 300 to 350 pounds. But it was its appearance that was
mind-boggling. If Dr. Frankenstein took a warthog, a mas-
tiff, and a mountain lion and got about equal portions of
each cut off, then sewed them all together without looking
too closely or worrying much about where he placed the tails

or the mane or stuff like that, then he might have come up with something like the animal that roared in the highway dead ahead and exhibited jaws that would make Godzilla get dentures.

If it thought it could stand up to an overloaded Harley going fifty miles per hour, then let it try. Stone shot ahead, aiming right at the thing. He gave it a long burst from the .50 caliber up front. But even as the slugs flew, the creature sprang to the side with the lightning speed of a cheetah. Stone breathed a sigh of relief as he shot past. Which was replaced by a gasp of horror within a split second as he heard the thing growl as they shot past—and then heard the damn dog behind him return the challenge. Stone felt the seat spring up, and he knew that the crazy Rambo of a dog had jumped into the fucking fray.

By the time he screeched the bike to a halt, he had gone another thirty feet. He slammed his booted foot out on the ground and swung the whole bike right around him. The match was already a blur of fur and howls and foam. Stone couldn't see what the hell was going on. He pulled up to within about ten feet and sat on the bike, his finger on the trigger, praying for a clean shot.

Suddenly the air cleared for an instant and Stone saw them both clearly, about five feet apart, looking at one another as if they wanted nothing more in this life than to tear the other one's face into noodles. And though Excaliber had taken on bears, lions, whole packs of dogs—and if he didn't always win, was at least able to walk away—at last it looked as if he had met his match. For the pit bull was already gored along one flank by the mutation's huge tusks, twelve inches long and standing on each side of its ugly face ready to gore again. And Stone could see as well that, though the dog had ripped its formidable teeth into the thing's throat area, it had no throat. The pit bull had ripped up some dark black neck fur but hadn't penetrated anything. There was nowhere on the damn thing to penetrate, as far as Stone could see.

Both animals reared back to have a second go at it. Stone

didn't have time to be chivalrous—or fair. Whatever the hell that meant. He got the atomically created thing in the sights of the .50-caliber and let loose with a stream of slugs that sliced into the mutant's stomach and chest. Even that seemed to hardly be enough. The thing lurched backward, snarling and creating quite a fuss as Excaliber stood back, his hair bristling and his jaws wide apart, snarling as he watched the mad dance of agony. But even the most armored of Mother Nature's monsters can't take a whole gutful of .50-calibers. And suddenly everything just exploded out of it and the animal collapsed in a bloody pile, its head jerking violently as its tusks dug into the road as if digging out a grave.

"Get up, you asshole," Stone snapped angrily as he pulled the bike alongside the dog. The pit bull glared up at him with its own anger as if to say, "You should have let me take the bastard on. I was just about to kick his ass. Didn't feel a thing, didn't feel a thing."

"Right," Stone snarled back as he looked at the dog's side. The tusk had gored about twelve inches along it. Not too deep, though, the pit bull was made of pretty hard materials himself. Stone released the throttle and the bike squealed around, the dog almost falling off as it clamped down hard with its legs. He drove hard, not looking back at the mountain of ugliness. He made a mental note not to come this way again.

It didn't take long for the warthog thing to die. Not that it couldn't have survived a few days falling to pieces if left on its own. But it wasn't left alone. Within minutes, the tubes with teeth were snaking down around the bottom of the crater where the still-twitching thing lay. Ordinarily its hide was too thick for the tubes to penetrate. But now it was shattered in places, blood spurting out in pulses as the heart beat on. The first of the tubes reached down under the thing, up into its still-living stomach, and clamped its rows of teeth around something. It pulled hard. The dying mutation let out a howl that even Stone and the dog heard, now two miles off. Then the rest of the snapping mouths closed in. And there were no more screams. Just the slurping sounds of dozens of the tubeteeth feeding, filling their underground stomachs with pools, reservoirs of blood, for when times got hard. When there was no blood to be had for love or money.

NINE

After the attack of the killer hog and the blood-drinking radioactive hoses with shark's teeth, the rest of the trip south to La Junta was relatively uneventful. Other than the road being nothing more than a series of holes for miles—which the wide-wheeled Harley didn't have all that much trouble with—Stone made good time. He was about ten miles from his destination when he decided to get off the interstate. He didn't necessarily want to announce his intentions until he knew just what the hell was going on. Riding in armed to the teeth was not the smartest way to find April—alive. He'd tried that route before. And nearly gotten his head blown off.

Stone headed down a one-laner that quickly changed from cracked asphalt to hard-packed dirt with rutted tire marks in some places. Just the kind of road he liked. The village traffic wasn't too likely to come by here. He had gone about two miles when he suddenly felt the skin crawl along the nape of his neck. Something was wrong. There were people near, very near. It was his intuition, the gift of the "Nadi," as the Indians who had saved his life when he had first left the bunker and nearly been killed had called him. And Stone's mental Distant Early Warning system was beeping full blast.

There were trees draping overhead all around them now. Vulnerable from the woods on each side—and the fucking air. "Great!" Stone spat out as he eased the Harley forward. If there was trouble, he had just allowed himself to ride right into a perfect ambush situation without even really realizing where he was going. Suddenly he saw faces just off the road ahead, about twenty feet inside the woods. About a dozen of them, all lurking around in the half-darkness, their faces fixed on him like cats' eyes in the night. Then—movement above him in the branches. His predictions of sky attack appeared about to become reality. More of the eyes, and the same sunken-looking faces, with scrawny arms hanging on around the branches as they peered down. And even as Stone reached for the 12-gauge and tensed his shoulders expecting one of the men to drop on him, he realized that no one was moving. No attack, no ambush was taking place, none whatsoever. For all the faces just kept looking at him with a blankness that Stone found quite unsettling.

He continued to take out the 12-gauge, but slowly now, and brought the bike to a complete stop with one hand. The dog was yawning behind him and making slurping sounds. But the sheer fact that the animal was not reacting to the men around them further confirmed Stone's feeling that they were no threat at all. For the canine's senses were tuned to a slightly higher level than Stone's. He had already found that out, rendering any thoughts of pride about his supposed extra abilities a mere joke.

As Stone surveyed the silent-as-a-morgue crew, he saw that, far from being a threat to him—or anyone—they were, in fact, pathetic-looking fellows, not dissimilar to pictures he'd seen of concentration-camp victims when they were released from Nazi camps after World War II. Skinny as rails with sores on their lips and faces, hopeless almost-dead looks in their eyes. He could see that they had gotten a miserable little sputtering fire going behind some bushes. And were toasting what looked like branches—to eat. Jesus Christ, what was this—the Home for the Hopelessly Depressed? These guys made Stone's blackest moments seem like he was watching a Laurel and Hardy movie. They had depression and apathy down to an art form.

Seeing that they meant absolutely no harm and, if anything, flinched as he trained his eyes on them, Stone dismounted and put back the shotgun. Didn't want to give anyone a heart attack. Not that they looked like they cared if they lived or died. The dog stayed on the back of the bike, stretching out to take up the full room and the warmth that Stone had left behind on the seat. He walked about ten yards over to the main group of the cadaverous-looking fellows, sprawled all around the small flame that passed for a fire. All in all, it was just about the most pathetic scene Stone had ever laid eyes on.

"Howdy," he said, walking up to within a few feet of the fire and addressing a man who sat in front of it, roasting one of the hard roots over the gasping flames. It didn't look as if it was getting cooked too fast. But a least this man, unlike the others, seemed to have a tiny spark of something left in his eyes.

"Hello," the man said back, slowly, as if he hadn't said the word for a long time.

"What the hell is going on here?" Stone asked, waving his hand around. "I mean, you guys look like you've been having a few problems. Not the least of which is that none of you are wearing more than a few stitches of clothes. Don't you know it's cold out?"

"Cold?" the brown-haired man said with a look of surprise. He looked around him, up at the sky and then down at his own shivering flesh, which was covered by a tattered sweatshirt that looked like it had been around at the turn of the century. "Yes, I guess it is cold, isn't it?" The guy looked intelligent enough, but he also looked as though he was about forty, and somehow, by his features, Stone knew he was hardly out of his twenties. They all were aged, drawn, broken. Like men who had been through some hellish experience, so terrible and destructive that there was hardly any life left in them—just shells with whatever had been a man either destroyed or hiding so far down inside of them that it was unseen and unwanted.

"Why aren't you clothed? Eating real food? Have shelters?" Stone asked them, exasperated, searching for some kind of emotional reaction, even anger. Their zombie-like state, all the faces just staring into the fire, not even looking up at Stone, was the worst thing of all.

"Shelter?" the man echoed back as if it were a word he had never heard before. "Oh, yes," he almost whispered. "Yes, warmth—and bed. I remember those things."

"That's great," Stone said, getting more and more pissed off by the whole scene by the minute. "You remember those things. What's wrong with him?" he asked, pointing at a guy who was lying flat on his back, naked, shaking violently with his hands twisted up in front of his chest like little claws. Foam was coming out of his nose and mouth.

"He was cleansed too long," the root cooker answered Stone. "There is nothing left up here." He pointed with his finger to his own skull, and for the first time there was a flicker of a dark smile, which zipped across thin lips before the face turned back to total rock again.

"What's your name, pal?" Stone asked.

"My name? My—name?" Again the man struggled within himself as if such thoughts were strange, difficult. "I am Terrance, Terrance Smythe. Yes, that's who I am."

"And I'm Stone," his interrogator answered with a grunt. "Well, I'm glad to see we're getting somewhere. Now, I don't mean to be nosy or anything," Stone went on, "but seeing as how you fellows don't seem engaged in very pressing business right now, maybe you could just tell me what happened to all of you—and what being 'cleansed' is?"

"Sure, I'll tell you," Smythe said, his face getting livelier than it had been thus far in their "conversation." "We are all rejects of the Cult of the Perfect Aura, which controls all of La Junta now. We—we . . ." He struggled again with the concepts, the words. Stone wondered if these suckers had exchanged even one word in the month before he'd arrived on the scene. "Guru Yasgar and the Transformer—they did this to us. They—make you drink things, and then make you do—horr—horr—" His voice choked up and he seemed to just stare straight ahead and stutter away for about ten seconds before he got through some terrible block in his mind. Whatever had been done to these bastards had been bad. Real bad.

"Horrible things to your mind, to your flesh. Many people go under the 'cleansing' and they become Yasgar's slaves, will do anything for him. He has hundreds, perhaps thousands of followers. We—we—couldn't be broken. Or rather..." He laughed with a snort as he looked around at his comrades and realized perhaps for the first time in a long time just how pathetic they all were. "At least, we couldn't be broken to fit the zombie type that Yasgar needs for his fucking slave city." Now Smythe was starting to get angry as his memories sprang back, as his broken shell still found one more little spark of fire. Good, Stone thought, good. Anger was the only thing that could bring these husks of men back to life.

"So they dumped us, just dropped us in the woods to die, to starve. As many have. We are the Broken Ones. We live just to die. But most of them... their heads just don't work right. Can hardly even crap without shitting on themselves. I'm probably the Einstein of the bunch." The man laughed again, revealing that every single tooth in his mouth had been broken. Nice guy, this Yasgar. And somehow Stone knew that the bastard had his sister.

"Most who come here in the woods have died. I pull them back behind the trees over there. Some of these Broken Ones you see around you—they tried to eat the corpses. But I wouldn't let them. There are some things even the lowest of men must not stoop to."

"Well, that's good to hear," Stone said. At least the guy still had a conscience. That was more than a lot of men possessed these days. "This guy Yasgar, you ever see him?" Stone asked, wanting to know the description of the man so he'd know who to kill when he found him. Stone's blood was coming to a slow boil over all this. It disgusted him to see his fellow man fallen to such a state.

"Yes—I—I—I—," Smythe stuttered again. There were so many terrible memories locked in that head. And every question that Stone asked seemed to bring them out. "I saw him several times. He is—is—is—fat, very fat. And has black eyes that look right through you. He wears a black robe that floats over him, not even touching his skin. His voice is like thunder. I tell you, Stone, Guru Yasgar is not a a man at all, but a beast from hell, sent here to destroy mankind." Suddenly the man was ranting and raving and rose up in his place, letting the root fall into the coals and smolder with a sour oily smoke.

"Easy, pal, easy," Stone said, slapping him on the shoulder. "I'm on your side. You want to get back at this bastard, maybe I'm the man to talk to." Suddenly he heard a rustling of leaves just above his head and looked up to see one of the Broken Ones hurtling down, his arms and legs all flailing about like a rag doll. Just by the clumsy fall, Stone knew the poor bastard wasn't even trying to attack—he had just slipped. Stone managed to shift his body quickly out of the way and throw his arms out, actually catching, or at least slowing, the emaciated man's body. It sort of bounced off his arms and chest and then dropped to the leaf-covered ground with a loud groan. The man rose up to a kneeling position, apparently none the worse for wear.

Stone looked down at him with disgust flickering across his face. "Shouldn't climb trees, pal, if you don't know how to hang on." The man just looked at him like an orphan staring through a window.

"Oh, Jesus," Stone muttered under his breath.

"They climb the trees because they are afraid," Smythe said, now standing and facing Stone. "They have no weapons, are too weak to fight. When wolves or wild dogs come in the night, they can't even fend them off. We all climb the trees after the fire goes out. See—look around you."

"All right," Stone said, clapping his hands together loud a

number of times so even the most comatose of them at least lifted his head at the sharp sounds. "It's boot camp time. You all just had the misfortune to run into Martin Stone— and I'm going to kick some energy into those dead asses of yours." Stone knew he was probably getting himself into something he was going to regret. But he had no choice. He was already starting to feel like a fucking mother hen to a brood of very messed up chickens.

TEN

"First thing," Stone said, addressing them as he paced around the fire, "is to get some shelters put up. It looks like it might rain. Ain't no way for a man to live, lying in the dirt, hanging on to tree branches. Now, let's get some asses in gear here," Stone yelled, walking around, grabbing a branch, hitting it against a tree. But none of them seemed all that enthusiastic about getting up and doing much of anything.

"It's night, mister," Smythe said. "Animals crawling around. They's all scared at night." He pointed around to the huddled masses, who were like a bunch of corpses stacking themselves up so as to make it easier for death to collect them.

"Listen, gang," Stone said, turning around to all of them, who watched warily. "You boys ain't got a hell of a lot to do tomorrow morning, so it ain't gonna hurt you to do a little work now." Moans and hisses filled the flickering shadows around the slowly falling fire.

"Numero uno—if you're scared of animals," Stone said, walking off a few paces and grabbing some branches that had fallen from a dying tree, "is make a bigger fire." He threw the dry wood onto the flames and they quickly shot up into the air. The men looked on in amazement. The event seemed like some sort of supernatural occurrence. But they quickly took advantage of the fire, banding together, edging toward the warming flames, rubbing their hands and legs as they tried to get some heat into their bones for the first time in a long time.

Stone whistled toward the bike. He was going to need some additional motivation. The pit bull yawned, stretched itself several times, and then jumped down and came out of the darkness, stopping at Stone's feet. The men reacted instantly to the dog. And didn't like it at all. They had had too many dog packs come in the night and eat a number of their own to make them particularly enamored of the species. Stone would used that fear to his—and their—advantage, though they didn't know it.

"Now move, fellows. My dog here doesn't like to get wet when it rains or snows. And when he gets angry, I don't like to see the results." He kicked the pit bull in the side and it let out a snarl, baring its teeth and looking around to see who the hell was fucking with it. But the Broken Ones were already up on their feet. Even the ones who couldn't walk were dragging themselves off. Everybody was moving except the dead—of which Stone counted three out of a total of twenty-six.

"Good, you're moving," he yelled out to them. "That's an excellent start. Now, grab whatever big branches you can find—long and thick enough to hold up for a while. You understand me?"

"Yes," a few voices grudgingly hissed back. Stone pushed the dog forward, giving it a good shove with the bottom of his boot. Again the animal looked around at him as though he was completely mad and it was contemplating whether to take the boot down to the pins or not. But the movement of the Broken Ones caught its attention and the pit bull pranced along and up to a bunch of them. Though the animal was just being friendly and wanted to get petted and play a little, the half-mindless men saw only a demon dog, a flesh ripper, and they moved fast. Within minutes

Stone had a whole little depository of wood stretching around him. Already their eyes were open wider, their lungs breathing deeper. Against their goddamn wills, Stone was going to give them the instant twelve-hour course in how to be men.

"Very good, very good," Stone said. They seemed to like the praise, and a few of their faces broke out into childlike smiles, like a baby that had just deposited its first turd in the porcelain bowl instead of bed. Stone was working only with the highest-quality material here, there was no doubt about it.

"Now, Smythe, why don't you get the next-strongest guy around here and drag these three bodies out of here. Take them at least a hundred yards. And then I want them buried. At least three feet down, so the animals don't get them. Probably the main reason you've been getting all these damn blood packs sniffing around the place is that you're allowing corpses to just lie among you. Jesus Christ—get some sense into those overwashed brains." They looked at him as if they were trying to listen, trying to understand. But from the tongue-hanging, drooling expressions of most of them, Stone could see he was working with prekindergarten mentalities. Ninety percent of the helpless sons of bitches had Jello for brains.

Stone took four of the strongest branches and had the men dig holes about twenty feet apart. He ordered four of them to take each corner and slam the posts in, then fill them in with mud. Though the men were simpleminded and worked slowly, under Stone's constant direction and supervision, telling each little group of them where to take what piece of wood, where to drag what bucket of water and mix it with dirt, they started actually getting things done. Within an hour of Stone's arrival, the place was a regular beehive of activity.

Once the main frame was completed Stone showed them how to lay the cross pieces, tying them down at each end with vine and then building a cross foundation with smaller

branches. Again, they caught on once they had a visual dem-
onstration. They seemed to think it was fun, with all of them
wanting to participate now as if it was some kind of game.
Even the crippled ones crawled around underneath weaving
in small branches to help make the roof dry. Another hour
produced a woven lean-to that looked for all its twisted un-
evenness fairly strong—and well designed. The angled roof
would push off the rain; the mud-cemented corner beams
would keep the thing strong enough to take any but the
strongest winds. Now for the mortar. Stone directed them to
make thick buckets of mud and then pour them over the
walls and roof, mixing in leaves and twigs to form an almost
impenetrable natural barrier to the elements. Again, slow at
first, once they saw that all that it entailed was mixing mud
and playing pat-a-cake with the roof, they contributed.

Once Stone saw that the whole mud-splashing operation
was well under way, he gathered the pit bull, Smythe, and
one other fellow who he had observed to be a cut above the
rest. Which wasn't saying a hell of a lot. Still, the man
didn't drool, could talk—if only softly—and had a little
more muscle on his wasted body than the rest. He'd have to
do. Stone took them out as the others worked on. The night
had fallen black as a velvet sheet, with just a few stars and
the glow of the universe to guide them through the woods.
Smythe and the second man, who called himself only,
"Damaged," were extremely reluctant to come along, to go
into the shadows where they had heard the screams of their
fellows. But with Excaliber taking up the rear and showing a
few teeth when they slowed down, and Stone taking the lead
holding the Ruger .44 in his hand, safety off and ready for
quick fire, they had no choice.

They had to learn how to fend for themselves. And fast.
Stone didn't say a word, just led them through the forest
until they came to a rise, with a large flat boulder atop it. He
led them up to it and then lay down prone on his stomach
and pointed that they should do the same. The dog got down
on its haunches alongside him and looked down toward the

large meadow below them, stretching off for nearly a half-mile in each direction with trees at the end. Smythe began to complain that he "didn't know a whole lot about hunting," but Stone just put his fingers to the man's lips.

"Look—just watch me!" The two of them watched sullenly as Stone whistled softly twice to the dog and then slapped it on the side. The animal shot down the side of the boulder, dropping down the eight-foot face to the meadowland below. Like a rocket, it tore ass straight away from them and headed for the woods on the far side, just a gray mass of shadows. Stone held the pistol in his outstretched hand and breathed out hard, getting his arm and body as relaxed as possible. Then he waited.

They didn't have to wait long. The dog had been gone less than two minutes when there was a commotion from out of the trees and suddenly they could see a large shape coming straight at them as if its tail was on fire. At first it wasn't clear just what it was. But then, as a mass of thick clouds passed overhead and the stars suddenly splashed down over them inundating the scene with a billion pinpoints of light, they could see exactly what the dog had flushed out. A buck —and a big one at that. A good six feet at the skull, with horns on each side that looked as if they could make good chair frames. Behind the thing the dog was racing up a storm, snapping and barking and putting on quite a show, considering the buck was much larger than it was.

Stone waited until the animal was within about fifty yards, and pulled the trigger twice. The two men next to him let out little whelps of fear from the sharp retorts. But the buck did a lot more than just make sounds. It stopped dead in its tracks as two red holes the size of silver dollars appeared in its skull. The thing rose up on its back legs, did a little dance to some unheard beat, and then fell right over on its back, one of its horns sticking into the turf as it wiggled around in its death throes.

"Jesus, Jesus," Smythe kept mumbling under his breath.

The rapid-fire events of the evening were apparently a little too much for him to take in one sitting.

"Come on," Stone said, reholstering the Ruger and jumping down from the rock. They followed behind, their stomachs growling as they approached the game. Excaliber had stopped and was pointing at the buck. Smythe and Damaged got down on their knees and leaned over to begin drinking, lapping at the blood that was collecting below it.

"No!" Stone shouted, pulling both of their shoulders back so they didn't have a chance to drink. "Men do not drink blood like animals! We will cook the buck, and eat like civilized beings—not savages." He knew they were incredibly hungry, could hear the stomachs making all kinds of gurgling sounds. But still, they had to learn certain things. At least as long as Stone was on the scene, the men would not drink up blood like a hyena on their hands and knees.

It took them about fifteen minutes to drag the carcass back to camp. And Stone was glad to see, when they pulled the thing into the Broken Ones' village, that the rest of them had just about finished the roof and walls of the hut. They continued to pour unending amounts of mud over it, not really knowing when to stop. The mud would just protect them a little longer from being washed off by each storm.

All of their eyes went wild with hunger as the meat was hauled in. But again Stone kept them back, and first skinned, drained, and then butchered the animal, showing them all how to do it. They watched, fascinated and starving, as his razor-sharp Bowie blade ripped through the meat as if he was in the back room of a supermarket. With the fire higher now, Stone took a whole bunch of select steaks and organs and slammed them onto spits over the flames. The sound of twenty or so stomachs gurgling ravenously by the fire was not the greatest appetizer. Nor were the whinings of the pit bull, which looked at the sizzling meat with the expression of a priest spotting God in the very heavens.

After a few minutes, when the meat was cooked enough to kill any disease, bacteria, whatever, Stone gave them the go signal. It was as though a stampede of lions had been let into the arena to devour the Christians. He grabbed his own stick up and barely got out of the way in time. And if the gurglings had been a little disgusting to Stone, the rippings and tearings, the splatterings, the faces coated with blood and half-chewed meat, like werewolves at Gristedes, made Stone turn away and chew his smoking ribs behind a tree.

ELEVEN

When Stone got up the next morning at the stroke of dawn, the first thing he had them all do was clear out of their newly constructed home, which in the dim light of the coming day looked almost respectable. Then it was exercise time, to get their watery blood sloshing around inside them. They groaned and complained, but they more or less followed along. Even the legless cripples slapped their hands together and rolled around on the ground trying to get into the spirit of the whole thing. And that, after all, was what mattered. Spirit.

Stone could see, as the burning scalp of the sun poked up over the tree line, that they already looked slightly healthier. A touch more flesh on the bones after all the meat they'd eaten last night. Half the buck was gone, and it had been big. Still, he had no illusions that he had done anything more than stave off their decline into complete savagery. He headed over to the fire and saw that at least Smythe had kept it going. He and a few others were still slicing up pieces of the beast, toasting them over the flames on spits as Stone had shown them. They seemed to have a hunger that had no bounds. He understood why.

Stone made an instant decision and went to his bike, took

out a small bundle, and walked back over to Smythe, who stood up as he approached.

"I'm giving you this, man," Stone said, handing the skinny fellow a .38 snub-nosed revolver that he had stashed in one of the boxes on the back of the bike—just in case. Just in case was here now. "And a box of ammo. That's almost a hundred shots. Make 'em count. You can keep this bunch fed for a while, anyway. You hear what I'm saying?"

"I hear you, Stone," Smythe replied with a look of awe as he took the weapon. With this he could get them much food, could protect them at night. It changed their whole world in an instant. From one of constant fear and hunger to one of possibility, however minute it might be.

"Do you know how to use it?" Stone asked, not wanting to embarrass the guy, but not wanting to leave him unable to operate the thing.

"Yes, yes, I do, Stone. I had a pistol many years ago, on my father's ranch. Before . . . before—"

"Easy, easy," Stone said, putting his hand on the man's shoulder. Smythe strapped the holster on around his waist and took out the pistol. He aimed it at a rotten stump of a log about forty feet off and squeezed the trigger. The gun erupted with a sharp burp and the Broken Ones around him pulled back, oohing and aahing in fear and excitement. The slug hit the bottom of the stump and sent a whole little cloud of ground-up wood into the air. Not bad.

"You should be able to bag something," Stone said. "Now remember, save your ammo. And have the other men flush out the prey like the dog did. Send them into the woods, make noise, bang things, whatever. And then wait in a field outside. You can't miss. It's what hunters have been doing since caveman days."

"Thank you, Stone," Smythe said in a whisper as he slid the gun back into the holster. He had felt like a piece of dried-up spit just the morning before. And now. . . . This one man had changed things beyond dreams. It was impossible, and yet—

"Just one favor for me, " Stone said as he took the man

around a tree so the others couldn't hear. There was no sense in trusting anyone more than he had to. It seemed unlikely that there would be spies among these. But the one thing Stone had learned about the new America was you never knew what was going to happen next, and that enemies lurked behind the softest of flowers.

"I want to leave my bike here. We'll push it back out of sight into the woods. But I need you to guard it, keep an eye on it, make sure none of your brain-cleansed pals here get a hankering to start chewing on the leather or something."

"No, Stone!" Smythe said firmly. "Those days are gone. I will not let these men, as you say, be less than men. At least while I'm here. And this is here." He patted the gun. "I'll watch the bike, sure. Me and Damaged can cart it off."

"I'd rather keep it out of town," Stone explained. "My ace in the hole. Because I have to go into what you all came out of. My sister is in there."

"God help her," Smythe whispered, crossing himself with his hands. "And you, friend," he added softly as he put out his hand and gripped Stone's arm.

"Come on, dog," Stone yelled, whistling for the mutt, which was needless to say over on the meat line for breakfast. The animal was chomping down the meat as fast as it could be cooked up. The man who was doling out the sizzling meat didn't dare refuse. Not with these almond eyes focused on him. The dog swallowed down its last helping fast when it heard Stone whistle, and then grabbed another piece that must have weighed a good five pounds. The pit bull dragged it along as if it just happened to be attached to its mouth, and came up alongside Stone.

"We're moving, dog," he said, looking down as the animal chewed wildly away. Stone took one last look at the chomping encampment of mental cases as they sat around the fire. Well, he'd done all that he fucking could. He wasn't God. He saw Smythe and Damaged taking the bike off into the woods as he turned and started down the back road toward La Junta. He hoped he could trust them. But Stone had basically been trusting his intuition up until now. There was no sense in stopping now. At least he was still alive. Which was more than a lot of men could say.

He walked quickly along the dusty road as the sun rose up into the sky like a flaming basketball searching for a new position among the high puffy clouds. The dog followed behind, still gulping down every last meat flake it could. They walked for nearly an hour and a half at a fast gait. Wildlife rushed off as they approached. They didn't pass any cars. Just one of the same walking-dead type, his clothes hanging in shreds over him as he walked by, his eyes focused on infinity. Maybe the poor bastard would find the others down the road; if not . . . well, maybe it was better to just go out fast. Before you discovered you no longer had a mind.

Then the town of La Junta was suddenly right before him as he come over a slope and looked down. It was spread out over acres, mostly low-built structures, all crude log-cabin-type construction. A few larger buildings here and there, including a nearly-four-story-high, very elaborately and peculiarly decorated one, like some sort of mix between American Pioneer and twelfth-century Hindu. Stone headed down the slope, a little more slowly now, as he wanted to take in everything carefully. There wasn't going to be room for mistakes here. He pulled Excaliber close to his leg, telling the dog in no uncertain terms to stay close, stay cool, and be ready to go for the jugular.

He had barely set foot in the town when Stone did a triple take. For coming around the side of a log building was an elephant. It was pulling an immense tree behind it that was attached to a chain wrapped around its trunk. Excaliber made a strange sound deep in its throat. It had never seen anything so big. Stone and the canine waited until the thundering beast had hauled the multiton tree past them and down a side street. Stone could see already that the people here were in better shape than the Broken Ones out on the road. At least on the outside. These had pink cheeks, and their clothes weren't torn. But their eyes, as he walked by more of them, were just as vacuous. Perhaps more so. For these were all smiling. Dumb painted-on smiles sat on every face like the superexaggerated expressions of the old smile buttons, the demise of which was to Stone one of the positive benefits of the collapse of American civilization.

"Good day. May your aura be always blue," a man said as he passed by, tilting his head slightly as if bowing. His eyes blazed with good cheer, but Stone could see it was all a lie. There was nothing behind those eyes or the lips. Just a recording somewhere in what was left of the man's brain, telling him to utter the words.

"Good day," Stone replied, "and your aura too." Everyone he passed nodded with the same little tilt of the head, the same words, everything. It was as though they had come from the same mold. Every one of them. He came to a corner, turned, and walked down another block—and encountered the same greeting from every man and woman he passed. He saw two more elephants, which seemed to do all the heavy work around the place; Stone couldn't see a single motorized vehicle. The citizens all wore the same sort of gray suit, sort of like the old Nehru style of the sixties, with simple lines and cut-off collar. It made them all appear to be robots, like something out of Red Guard China. Every one of them seemed so alike in clothing and manner it was spooky.

Suddenly there were three of them blocking his path. They didn't act menacing, but clearly wanted to have a few words with him before he took another step. These had robes on, a brownish-red color, and were clearly of a higher rank than the others. It wasn't that they didn't look spaced out as well, but their eyes had at least a glint more intelligence in them, their mouths moved a little more freely. Apparently this Yasgar had different levels of mind control. Only problem was, the more control, the less mind. So he must have had to compromise. That meant that the more intelligent ones might be more open to persuasion—or threats. Stone filed the information away under "Ultra Important." And promptly forgot it.

"Hello, welcome to the Town of the Perfect Aura," one of

them said. "It is a lovely day, isn't it?" The three strained faces looked at Stone questioningly.

"Yes, yes, it sure as hell is a lovely thing to be here in this lovely town on a lovely day like this," Stone replied with as exaggerated a smile as the others had. The three men tried to smile even wider than he, and Stone wondered whether their mouths were going to split.

"And what might your purpose be here in our fine town, stranger?" the same gray robe asked.

"Oh—just vacationing." Stone smiled back. "Heard you had some real good guru or something here, preaching a whole lot of gospel. I'm a man of God, so I come down from the mountains—to see just what was going on. Any man who preaches the Lord's work—well, that man is someone I want to hear. Amen," he added, looking down as if in prayer.

"So you've come to hear about the Perfect Aura. That is a wonderful thing," the man said. "We have all experienced the healing pureness of the Aura, have tasted the nectar of transformation. It is a miraculous thing indeed. You must come to our Ceremony of the Golden Elixir tonight at the Auric Temple. All are welcome, all strangers are welcome."

"Even animals," one of them added sweetly, as if syrup were dripping from his tight lips. He reached down to pet Excaliber, who let out a menacing growl and backed off, his fur rising up slightly. The dog clearly didn't like any of this crew, not one bit. It didn't know what was wrong. It didn't particularly care what was wrong. Just that there was something out of sync with them. Like a broken car that you wouldn't sit in from the sheer sounds of its malfunctioning engine.

"Ah, isn't he cute," one of them said. "Our Guru loves animals. And they love him. They flock to him like the legendary St. Francis of Asissi."

"Oh, isn't that nice," Stone said, hoping he wouldn't puke over all these "nices and wonderfuls." "I do hope your Guru will be at the temple tonight so I can meet him personally," Stone said, reminding himself to make sure his .44 and autofire 9mm Beretta were fully loaded.

"Yes, the Guru and the Priest of Transformation will be there," one of them said, laughing as if the thought of his absence were completely absurd. "He *must* be there. That is the whole ceremony. It is he who leads us into the purity of the mind, the nectar of the flesh."

"Sounds great, I'm telling you. I'm glad I came down here already. It's just what I've been looking for up in them mountains. Nectar of the flesh, paradise of the brain. Now, those are the kind of things a practical mountain boy like me would pay a pretty penny to get his grubby hands on." Stone laughed, the cultees laughed, even the dog seemed to laugh, letting out a little bark and stretching its own mouth a little farther back. Never had so many lying smiles been flashed so intensely by so many mouths in such a small space. It would have made the Guinness World Book of Lies—if there were such things anymore.

TWELVE

Everywhere he walked, Stone was greeted by the smiling, blank-eyed faces. There were other outsiders around town, Stone could see as he moved deeper toward the center of town. La Junta had a thriving salt and fur business along with a number of other small stores. Apparently there was a certain amount of free commerce in and out of the place. But by God, the cultees sure as hell came on strong to all passersby.

"Your aura needs cleaning," a couple of bright faces said as Stone walked on.

"Thanks—I'll drop it off at the laundry," he answered without stopping.

"Happiness is just an inch away," a pimply-faced teen spoke up in front of him as Stone tried to avoid him.

"And nirvana is just a silly millimeter longer." Stone smirked back. But he didn't slow down. Once you slowed for a cultee, they were on you like a wolf on a corpse. First the guts, then the brain and heart. They attacked from every direction. Even the dog let out a growl now and again as they approached, which seemed to work quite well as a defensive maneuver. For these here, like the men out in the woods, didn't seem to like dogs too much.

As he walked along the main street, Stone was amazed at

how many little stores there were. More than most towns these days had, to say the least. These people sure as hell were an industrious lot. Suddenly he heard some drums, some kind of commotion up about a block ahead, and he walked a little faster. A crowd was gathering as he came up and he heeled Excaliber in closer to his leg, not wanting there to be any trouble. It was drums—of a sort—huge tin washtubs upside down, being banged on with long sticks. It made quite a sound. But it was the sight that impressed him.

For down a ramp in front of one of the larger log buildings, an elephant was being led out by one of the robed figures. Stone watched in amazement as he felt the pit bull tense up by his leg. The animal didn't like things that were a hundred times bigger than it was. It made it feel insecure. The huge beast was led right up to the center of the square, where Stone could see as he craned his neck over the now-crowded street in front of him there was a man down on his knees kneeling in front of a large wooden block. Stone started getting a sick feeling in his stomach.

"This man stole from the Temple of the Perfect Aura," a robed figure was bellowing out as he paced around the kneeling, crying man. "He took what belonged to Guru Yasgar—and to the entire community of believers." There were murmurs and chatter among the crowd, about half of whom were cultees, the other half outsiders, at least as far as Stone could make out.

"He took the Golden Nectar—and sold it to outsiders as a crude beverage to get them drunk," the robed man, whose face Stone couldn't quite see as the oversize brown robe kept flowing around him, billowing around his face and body so he was always in shadowy motion, just a blur without real features. "Nothing can be so blasphemous—other than an attack on the Guru himself. For this." The robed man paused and held up both hands dramatically. He wanted the crowd to get a good show. This was, after all, for their benefit. Should some other madman get the idea to steal anything—even a paper clip from the Temple—they would meet the fate that was quickly approaching this hapless sobbing slob.

Though the man hardly seemed to know who, or where, he even was. He had the same semiretarded kind of look that Stone had seen on most of them now. It was hard to believe that the fat little slug could have even planned out a whole thievery and sale operation. But whoever ran the show had their reasons for what they did. And though Stone didn't know what the motivation was, he suddenly realized what the punishment would be. And he wished he hadn't eaten so much meat at breakfast that morning.

"Put your head down on the block," the gray robe commanded.

"No, no," the bound slug pleaded, his face covered with grease and snot, his mouth a dribbling stream of saliva.

"Down, worthless cur," the robed man screamed again, and this time walked over to the kneeling man and kicked him hard on the back and neck, forcing him down though it took a good dozen blows. The man's head was now down sideways on a yard-wide square of wood. The robed man raised his hand and the handler began leading the animal forward the few yards toward the victim. There was a sudden silence throughout the entire crowd in which you could hear a pin drop—or at least the footsteps of an elephant. The handler led the mammoth beast right up to the wood and then tapped the elephant on the right leg. It lifted the leg high, a good six feet in the air.

"Down," the handler said, "down!" and tapped the beast's leg with a stick. The elephant's chair-size foot came down fast and made contact with the head. It was a grisly sight, which repulsed Stone—but he couldn't tear his eyes away. The elephant dug down hard, like a smoker stamping out a cigarette, and the head just sort of crunched beneath it, exploding out suddenly. The face, the hair, everything just disappeared as it all shattered and shot out from beneath the elephant's crushing foot like an egg in a blender. The elephant pushed all the way down and then turned the foot several times until it was completely flush against the wood.

"Up," the handler commanded, and the great gray leg

lifted again. The elephant pulled back and stood there surveying what it had wrought.

"Yes . . . see—this is what befalls those who betray Yasgar. This!" the gray robe shouted. He walked around the block, pointing down. Not that you needed to look all that close to see that there was nothing left above the shoulders than a paste that wouldn't have been enough for a good soup stock. The body of the dead man slid down the slide of the block and lay on the street. It didn't even twitch, so dead was it.

Suddenly the elephant reared back as a crow shot down and pecked at the flakes of skin on the wood block, frightening the big beast. The handler snapped a stick against the creature's side, and the hood flew back. Stone gasped in simultaneous horror and joy. It was his sister. It was April who was handling the elephant. It was his sister who was the executioner.

"Jesus, God," he muttered, forgetting in spite of all his training exactly where he was—and what was going on for a few seconds. For he suddenly circled around the back of the crowd and came up to her through the masses just as she got the great beast quieted down.

"April—April, it's me, Martin! What have they done to you? What—"

She stared at him with cold, dead eyes.

"Oh, Jesus, you're—one of them," he gasped in horror.

"Yes, Martin, I am," she answered mechanically with that same taut, lying smile that they all had. "And soon you will be too." She tapped the elephant on the trunk and stepped back. Suddenly the animal whipped around and grabbed him in its trunk, instantly lifting him twelve, fifteen feet in the air as it shook him this way and that. Stone felt like a bean in a baby's rattle, as if his brains were being pounded within his skull to the consistency of porridge.

He saw the gray robe approach her. And they were both looking up at him, the man smiling, then laughing as the elephant shook Stone this way and that so that the whole world was flying by around him as if he was in a washing machine. Then it lifted him suddenly very high so he must have been nearly twenty feet up—and then dashed him quickly down again, releasing Stone as its trunk was pointing straight out, so Stone flew through the air and crashed into the cracked pavement of the street. There was a loud honking sound as the elephant trumpeted out its powers. And then Stone was slammed into a darkness that didn't feel good at all.

THIRTEEN

When Stone came to, he was coughing up a thick sticky liquid that was being poured down his throat. He coughed violently, as they'd given him a lot, and the hacking woke him suddenly from the black pool he'd been floating in. Shapes were dancing around him, dozens of them. Robed, so he could see only their bare feet running around him on a wooden floor. He looked down and saw that he was tied hand and foot to a pole, standing in an upright position. His clothes were still on, but his boots were gone and—

"My dog," Stone sputtered suddenly, looking into the face of the black-robed figure who stood a few yards in front of him. "Where's my fucking dog?" He began yelling. If the bastards had done anything to Excaliber, he'd . . . he'd. . . . He'd what? He couldn't even move more than an inch in any direction. The black-robed man raised his arm and the robe draped off of it, making it look like a skeletal arm was pointing at him. Two nearly unclad women in jewel-encrusted loincloths and minuscule silver cups over their melon breasts came forward and held a large golden goblet up to Stone's mouth.

He tried not to take any in—but they just kept pouring it, and as he at last gasped in for air, Stone took in one, then several more mouthfuls of the stuff. He could feel it already.

A hot tingling sensation that ran from his tongue right down his gullet. Whatever the hell it was, it tasted fiery, wonderful in a way. And he knew something else—it was drugged with enough junk to put King Kong on the floor drooling. Within seconds Stone could feel his vision getting blurry, with an almost golden haze to it.

"Ahh, you feel it now, do you not?" The black-robed figure spoke, and Stone swore that the man was God, the way his voice thundered into his ears. It was as if he were inches from a thousand-watt amplifier. The black-robed figure raised both arms to the ceiling, which, Stone noticed as he followed the motion, seemed to be painted with things—angels, demons, dragons? He couldn't see clearly, because the room was lit by only a few oil lamps around the walls and candles that some of the dancing figures carried in their hands. Stone thought his mind felt as if it was a rubber band and it was being pulled in about five directions at once.

Suddenly it was as if lightning bolts were coming down from the ceiling and into the robed figure's fingers. The man stood up straight, and though Stone couldn't see any features beyond an ugly bunch of shadows, he could see the two glowing ruby-red eyes within. They weren't the eyes of a human. Even in his increasingly drugged mental state, Stone at least knew that much.

"I am the Transformer, the High Priest of the Perfect Aura," the black-robed figure bellowed out. Again, to Stone's ears it sounded as though a jet plane was taking off. His brain hurt from the sound, burned as if nails were being driven into it. And even as he tried to focus his eyes, two women danced their way forward, writhing like belly dancers, and poured yet more of the golden liquid into his lips.

"You have been chosen as one of the lucky ones, to have your aura changed from black to blue, from depression and pain to happiness, bliss and—order." The eye glowed ever redder beneath the enclosing hood. Stone got a blurred glimpse inside for a flash. He saw what looked like the face of a man long dead—not yet a skull, but definitely no longer a living being either. The muscles were all twisted, the skin brown and rotted in places. Stone felt as if his skull was going to explode.

"Man is imperfect," the Transformer said. "His aura is dark and riddled with pain."

"His aura is dark," the dancing robed figures screamed back as they all circled faster around Stone, closing in, whirling like tops as they waved their gray-robed arms around in front of them like windmills. Stone could feel that he was falling into some deep spell, almost a coma. Everything was already golden with a haze, as if he was looking at an old photograph instead of real people.

"The Perfect Aura is golden—that is why we drink the golden liquid." He pulled out a cup of his own and lifted it to his lips. Stone heard a slurping leathery sound come from within the hood and then the Transformer threw the goblet across the room. "Perfection is no fear."

"Perfection is no fear," the dancing robes screamed back, now reaching a frenzy. Suddenly they pulled out skulls from beneath their robes and held them out in front of them in both hands. Stone gasped as they moved in closer, shooting around him almost at full run. The High Priest pulled back and stood just outside the revolving circle. The skulls danced and waved all around Stone's head, being slammed toward him, coming within inches of his face.

"There is no death. There is no life," the Transformer screamed, raising his hands. And Stone swore he saw sparks shooting out of the tops of them. Although just how much he could vouch for the accuracy of what he was seeing, he wasn't placing any bets on. For even as he drifted into some weird places in his brain, Stone, or at least some part of him, knew that he was on drugs. That this wasn't real. Wasn't all real. Or was it?

The Nectar hit him more, and he felt his whole body turning to rubber, without sensation, his mind becoming like an infant's or a savage's mind, no longer able to judge or even think, just watch and feel terror and fear and. . . . The skulls seemed to smile now too, and chattered to one another and to him, their teeth slamming open and closed as they flew complex patterns in the air all around him. It might have gone on for seconds, minutes, or even years for all Stone knew. He completely lost track of time, of anything except the blurred circle of skulls, eyeless sockets looking at him, screaming incomprehensible things in unknown languages.

Suddenly there was a great crashing sound like a thousand garbage cans being thrown off a rooftop, and as Stone tried to focus he saw that the skull-holding modern jazz dancers had pulled back into the shadows, where they continued to do a little two-step to a much slower tempo.

"There, you see—death is not an enemy. You must learn to dance with the monkey of death, with the gorilla of termination. Do you understand? Your aura is imperfect—I can see with my priest's eyes. We must correct that by draining you of all fear. As a leech drains the blood of disease, thus shall we drain the impurities of your mind, your soul."

"Soun's like jes' what I wuz lookin' fer," Stone managed to mumble, though his lips felt as though they each weighed about a ton. "Gettin' my aura leeched."

"Bring in the Death Lover," the High Priest screamed, and again Stone's ears felt as if they were about to come off their hinges. Either he was losing his hearing as well as his mind, or this fellow had been given a lung transplant from Godzilla. Stone's eyes managed to focus for a few seconds on a large wooden box that was being carried in from the shadows. Five robed men stood on each side of the seven-foot-long, three-foot-wide and -deep box as naked women with skulls on their heads danced around them seductively, hissing like animals in heat.

"Down," the Transformer commanded, pointing right in front of Stone. The robed carriers faced each other and lowered the thing. It was heavy, crude. And Stone could see, even in his brainless state, that it was a coffin.

"Open it," the Transformer ordered, his red eyes glowing like twin suns in the shadowy darkness of the twisted face. Hands reached down and pulled hard, and the top flew back.

And Stone gasped—even in his rubber-brained state he let out with a sharp sound as his jaw hung open. For inside the coffin was a woman. A dead woman, lying on a bed of royal purple velvet. The velvet was as perfect and smooth as the woman was ugly. He'd seen a lot of corpses in his day. But this one seemed to have been picked for an unusual state of repulsiveness, ugliness, with rot and worms and bugs and slimes all over the damn thing.

He felt his stomach start to heave, and he tried to hold back his rising lava of sickness.

"Yes, vomit it out," the Transformer commanded. "Vomit out your imperfect ways, spit up your poisoned aura. For now you shall find your new one, your golden aura. And she"—he pointed to the flesh-dripping corpse—"shall lead you down the path. She shall take your virginity of disease. She shall be your Death Lover." And as Stone looked down on the rotting pile of sludge that resembled a human in shape only, he did in fact upchuck much of the morning's meal. It splashed out over the corpse. The High Priest let him look at the thing for another minute or two as the drums began pounding again in the background. Then he raised those dreadful skeletal arms again and pointed at the box.

"Put him in," he said simply. The three most horrible words Martin Stone had ever heard. For even with enough drugs in him to take out a bear, he knew he didn't want a one-night stand with that. But it didn't appear he had a hell of a lot of choice. For suddenly hands were all over him, releasing him from the stake, untying his hands and feet. Stone clumsily tried to lash out. But he was so spaced out, his brain so unconnected to his body, that he just sort of flopped around like a puppet without a master as some of the dark faces even smiled at his ridiculousness. And even as he sputtered and felt his heart speed up as if it was doing wind sprints, Stone felt himself being placed down into the box with—it.

"Oh, Jesus, sweet Jesus," he mumbled under his breath over and over again, as if the words might somehow protect him from the filthy slime below.

"No—no more of the old religions," the High Priest commanded, walking around the coffin. "Now there is but one God—that is Yasgar. And there is but one truth—that of the Perfect Aura."

"The perfect aura," they all echoed, circling the box, shaking the skulls in their hands. Stone felt himself coming right down on the corpse woman, squashing into it. It was like mud, and it smelled like death itself, with a sickening putridity to it that threatened to make him heave again. And Stone could see, even as his drugged eyes opened slightly in horror, that it was coming up to kiss him. A kiss without lips, just worms, and eyes that looked lovingly at him and seemed to blink with lashes made of cockroach wings and pupils of maggot. Every part of him sank into her as they pushed down from above.

"Don't be shy." The Transformer laughed. "She is a good lover. She will take you where you want to go. She is completely uninhibited. In all ways the perfect woman. Close the box."

Words that Stone didn't want to hear. Hands appeared all around him even as he lay sprawled out on top of the dead thing like a man trying to mount a woman.

"No! No!" Stone screamed out as they closed the top and the flickering light of the oil lamps and candles around the room disappeared. And as they pushed it down, they pressed him closer into her, like an aunt trying to be a matchmaker. Such nice young kids. Martin Stone, with his brains and looks, and what's-her-name, so thin and always ready for action. Stone felt the top of the box grinding him into her so that she squished up all around him and began oozing over his legs and back. His lips were pressed right against hers, and because his hands were tied he couldn't even move. And as he sputtered and tried to breathe in air amidst the stench, a worm exited through the moldy porridge of her mouth and sought entry like an excited tongue into his.

Stone spat it out, and the thing flopped off down the melting face. He tried to pull back off the thing, away from her. But there was nowhere to go. Nowhere at all. And once the top was closed, they lifted the coffin and began dancing with it around the floor, shaking it and turning it this way and that as they screamed and banged on it. The motion of the turning made the corpse woman grab at Stone, her dead leathery mold-covered arms flapping all around him like a passionate woman giving her all, her fungus-covered thighs slapping opened and closed. And her face—nuzzling him, rubbing against his cheeks, seeking a kiss. A hot kiss for cold soupy lips.

FOURTEEN

Thus, Stone spent the night with a corpse. A first for him, but something he would have just as happily gone without. In a weird way the drugs saved him from total madness. They began hitting him so hard after about ten minutes that he fell into a semicoma, where his eyes closed and he sank into a state of deep breathing. Which, all things considered, was about the best he could have hoped for. The devotees on the outside continued their dancing and chanting, their skull-juggling, as they paraded around the room with the box long into the night. Then they placed the coffin in front of the altar so that the lovebirds could be alone together.

When the Transformer at last opened the box a good eight hours later, as the sun was just peeking through the glassless windows, Stone was looking straight up at him, his eyes open as much as the wearing-off drug would allow.

"I hope she don't have anything," Stone muttered as the robed face glared down. The face seemed to act confused for a minute as if trying to decipher what Stone had just said. Then he spoke.

"I see you are trying to be funny. That is not good. There is no humor in the state of the Perfect Aura. That means you are hanging on to your black aura ways. Fighting this world of perfection that we offer."

"I don't know what's wrong with me," Stone muttered. "I just don't want to join a club that makes me sleep with corpses."

"Then you must suffer the initiation of the Vermin Room. You must learn to give in, Stone, to submit. For you will join us sooner or later. All have. All—or die. It is just how much suffering and pain you wish to endure before you realize that perfection lies in the acceptance of your diseased state. And the surrendering to me of your mind."

"Hey, pal, you can have the rotten thing," Stone said, trying to force a brave smile, though he didn't feel too brave. If they were going to put him through something worse than this, he didn't want to be around to see it. Only, he was. "It hasn't done me a hell of a lot of good."

"You *say* that," the Transformer bellowed, his red eyes lighting up with rage. "But it is not what you believe. You are still filled with human failings. I can see them, can see right into your aura—completely twisted."

"I've got men coming," Stone lied. "Fifty of them, and they're tough as shit. They ain't going to like it if—"

"You lie, Stone," the High Priest barked within the shadows of the hood. "There are no others. You travel alone. We know more than you imagine about you. That is why we have chosen you to be an honored member of our society. I offer you nothing less than total freedom, freedom to soar above the chains of mortal man."

"Been fine this way up till now," Stone interjected. But he barely got the words out when they were pouring more of the golden liquid down his throat. He tried to shake his head, but with three of them holding him and two pouring it down, it didn't take long before he had swallowed a pint of the stuff. And just as his brain had been clearing, Stone suddenly felt it clouding up again, all fuzzy and rubbery. And though it took away some of the pain that he had begun feeling again in his leg, it also made him quickly lose track of where he was or what was going on.

"Over to the door," the Transformer commanded his underlings. Four of them carried the box with Stone still lying amidst the corpse sludge beneath him, hardly anything left of it now, as they had food-processed it through the night, with Stone as the blade. They came to a black circle in the floor, and the Transformer motioned for some of the robed lackeys to pull back the trapdoor hidden there.

"When next we meet," the Transformer hissed with reptilian darkness from the hood, "you shall have had your aura completely and totally cleansed. Of this I have no doubts."

"I gotta go," Stone drunkenly mumbled as he felt the golden liquid filling up his bladder. But apparently they didn't pay much heed to such requests, for suddenly the whole box was tilted over sideways and Stone felt himself tumbling out with the remains of slime falling all around him. He dropped for about ten feet into the darkness until he felt himself hit liquid, thick and foul-smelling. He gasped for air as some of the muck went into his mouth, but then discovered that though he had sunk in up to his chest he was standing with his feet on the bottom. At least he wasn't going to drown. The trapdoor overhead was slammed shut again and Stone let out a groan of horror, knowing already he wasn't ready for whatever was going to happen next.

The smell was the worst thing. It made him gag, catch his breath. It must have been a sewer, for nothing else could smell quite so thick, so foul. And as his eyes got used to the little bits of light trickling down through the uneven floorboarding above, where they were chanting, carrying out some sick ceremony or other, what he could see made Stone wish he were blind. For he *was* in a sewer—there were all kinds of wretched stuff floating around him. But worse than the aesthetics of the place—he wasn't alone. Spiders rushed up and down the walls, roaches, centipedes, all kinds of ugly little bugs slithering everywhere. There had been some insect buddies in the coffin—but *those* had been annoyances. There were enough here to eat him alive.

Though his hands and feet were tied, Stone was able to hobble around a little, careful as he could be. If he slipped and fell under the foul waves, he wasn't coming up again. And the thought of sucking in the stuff made him alert, his every drugged sense on full charge—or as full as they could get. He backed off to one of the corners of the chamber, where at least a little more of the light was cascading down from above. He squirmed into the corner so he was protected on two sides, and settled into place.

The additional helping of Golden Nectar they had forced into him was starting to really hit him now. And, Stone had to admit, in a way the stuff wasn't all that bad. It seemed to put a hazy kind of glow on everything, made him not care quite as much that he was just another turd floating in a sea of them. And he even sort of blissed out, his head half rolling around and nodding like some junkie on an Avenue D street corner. His eyes focused mindlessly on a single funnel of light that ran past him and disappeared like a spear into the black mud that was up to his chest.

He didn't know how many minutes he just stood there spaced out, but suddenly his attention was grabbed by splashing sounds. Stone turned his face around, and whatever pleasure the combination twelve-drug Mickey Finn was giving him vanished in a flash. For he was surrounded by bugs, bugs everywhere. On the mud-caked walls, on the rafters above, coming toward him in the water, scuttling along with multilegs. And the vague softness of the drugs suddenly turned hard and terrible. Stone felt a surge of paranoia sweep over him, making his heart palpitate a few times. It wasn't just the actual danger of the attack that was hard to judge so far, but the deeper unconscious fears that the drugs brought up in Stone. As they were supposed to do. Brought up his deepest fears, his infantile trembling terrors that had been pushed down for decades.

And suddenly the charging ranks of insects, spiders, centipedes, beetles, larvae, and things never catalogued by scientists appeared superhuge, immense, to Stone. Their jaws and claws and antennae looked like the appendages of monsters. In spite of himself, Stone let out a piercing scream as his heart seemed to turn to ice in his chest. Ten feet above, the Transformer allowed a razor smile to crease along his decomposing face. The "tough one" was losing his toughness fast.

Stone pulled himself farther back into the corner, rising up on his toes though his legs were getting that rubbery feeling, as if they might just go out from under him at any moment. He raised his bound hands up out of the slime, splashing a whole load of it over his face, though he hardly noticed. He just didn't want the bugs, swimming through the sludge ocean by the thousands, to get him. He splashed wildly in front of him, driving them back, sending them catapulting off onto the walls, where they slid back down into the foul waters and started back toward him once again. And Stone was right about one thing—he *was* being attacked. They hadn't seen such a meal as this for months. From every crevice, every little crack they poured, curious about all the splashing, the commotion, smelling food.

Stone had no idea how long he had been splashing away when he heard the door open above him and some objects were thrown down. They landed just feet from him, and as they bobbed to the surface, Stone's puffed eyes opened a notch wider. They were heads. Human heads, three of them, freshly chopped, for their flesh wasn't rotted at all, and their necks still oozed with the blood of the freshly killed. And under the weight of the drugs coursing through his system, Stone swore they were moving through the water, were coming at him, all of them, like demonic fish. And as they came, their eyes focused on him and their lips moved.

"Good day to you, sir. A fine morning it is indeed," said a bearded head with thick red lips.

"I think not," Stone whispered back. "I think it is an ugly, foul, shit-covered morning. And perhaps it is not even morning."

"Ah, Charles, I do believe he does not trust us," said another head, this one an old man with wrinkles covering every inch of his face, bobbing just inches to Stone's right.

"Goddamn right I don't trust you," Stone screamed out, starting to splash his hands again so that he forced the three heads back by the forces of the little waves he created. "You need a whole body for me to trust you," Stone exclaimed, which somehow in his drugged state made sense to him. A whole body. He sure as hell wasn't trusting just heads. It wasn't right. Though he wasn't quite sure why.

Then every fucking thing was coming at him—heads, centipedes, rats, spiders dangling down from above. And as they came they all spoke and argued, and it was as if he was in a madhouse. The madhouse of his own brain.

"Good day to you, sir," a black spider said as it landed on his forehead, took a big bite out of his scalp, and then quickly jumped off before he could react.

"Afternoon, mate," an English-accented waterbug whistled as it sidestroked through the black shitmud straight toward his lip. It tried to bite him, but Stone bit it first, cracking it in half and spitting out both pieces, which landed a few feet off in the water and were quickly gobbled down by hidden mouths from beneath the scummy surface.

"Like to get my teeth around that tail," said one of the bobbing heads, this one a female with lipstick still smeared on, as she spotted a rat coming toward Stone. She began snapping at it like a girl bobbing for apples at a Halloween party.

"You ass," the rat screamed back at the skull. "I'll rip out your mouth before you can bite me." Then the whole scene was melting and it all fell into complete madness. Everything was yelling and he was arguing about the nature of man and the universe with the skull of a week-old corpse and two rats who tore away at its rotted brain matter. If they couldn't win the argument with words, why, they'd just do it with teeth.

FIFTEEN

Stone didn't know where he was after that. It could have been hell for all he knew. Just stink and slime and things clawing and biting and his body shaking, his mind melting. Voices, screams. Then there was at last—light. And he was being hauled up out of the wretched place. He was put on the floor and buckets of water were splashed over him, cleaning off the slime, the filth that coated him. Then a brown robe was handed him to cover his nakedness. The Transformer stood before him.

"You are one of us now, aren't you?" the black-robed figure asked, the eyes glowing ruby-red within the hood.

"Yes—I—am one of you," Stone's lips replied slowly, though he didn't even know what the lips were saying. Somewhere inside Stone there was a sliver of his self left. A voice that screamed out that this was all a lie, that everything was wrong. But that voice was swallowed up, blanketed, buried, by the "cleansed" portion of his brain, the part that through shock, dehydration, and continuous doses of the Nectar had made Stone a mindless zombie.

"You took a long time, Stone," the High Priest said as he stood before the barely-able-to-stand brown-robed Stone. "An amazingly long time, far more than the others. But that is only because your mind was so cancer-ridden. Now you are free."

"Now I am free," Stone dumbly echoed. It was as if he had no will. How a bug or goldfish might have felt. The Transformer's words and face loomed in his mind like a god. And everything just drained away inside him when he tried to get up even the slightest mental resistance. He was at the bottom of a golden swamp, and for the life of him he was sinking deeper into it every second.

"Yes, now you are free," the Transformer said as he walked around Stone inspecting the man closely, looking into his eyes, then walking behind him and suddenly grabbing at his neck. Searching for a reaction, any quick or defensive motion. But there was none. Stone *had* been cleansed. It had taken five days down there in that filth, with constant dosings of the Elixir. The Transformer had thought he might just have to kill him after all—the first total failure. But Stone had started to succumb on the fifth day after he'd taken in quarts of the drug—enough to kill most men. Still, the High Priest made a mental note to keep the man heavily drugged at all times.

"Welcome to the Perfect Aura," the High Priest said, the rotted face within twisted in something approaching a smile. "Your new designation is Pod number 47. You are a brown robe of the fourth rank," the Transformer said, standing back and putting a golden chain around Stone's neck. At the end of the chain was a round locket with some symbols and the Guru's face carved into it.

"My name is Pod number 47," Stone repeated. "I am a brown robe of the fourth order."

"Yes, very good. Very, very good," the Transformer said approvingly as he stopped his close inspection, satisfied that Stone was in fact "cleansed." It was not something that could be easily faked. None had succeeded so far. The Transformer was a man of penetrating observation. Even the dilations of the pupils could betray a man. Stone was under. The glassy-eyed, lip-drooping expression that was on all his followers.

"Now, repeat after me," the Transformer said. "I, Pod number 47—"

"I, Pod number 47," Stone said, slurring his words, his lips hardly moving. He was so drugged out that his cheeks were hanging down the side of his face.

"Promise with my life and my blood—"

"Promise with my wife and my blud," Stone said, having trouble even following the words as he spun around somewhere inside his brain.

"To obey the Guru, the High Priest, and all the laws of the Perfect Aura."

"Obey my High Priest, the Guru, and all claws of Perfect Order," Stone echoed.

"And give my life to defend it."

"And give my wife to defend it," Stone said.

"You are now a full member of the Perfect Aura. And lucky for you, as so many out there in this barbarous land would give their right arm for such an honor."

"So lucky," Stone said as drool came down the corner of his mouth and dribbled down his chin and onto his nice new brown robe.

"Take him to the pod barracks," the Transformer commanded, and several of his robed underlings stepped forward and took Stone by each arm and toward the door. When he hit the light outside, Stone reeled back for a moment. He had been so used to the darkness, the slime, that the purity of a day with fresh sun streaming down was jarring, unpleasant to his drug-saturated system.

"Come," the two guards said. They pulled harder, and Stone was half dragged along the street and toward the far end of town. There were only other cultees here, as outsiders were confined to the commercial section of town. Each one that they passed bowed his or her head and said, "Good day. May the Perfect Aura shine down upon you." Which phrase was repeated by the two guards, and by Stone as well, who had trouble getting the words out. He imitated as well their mouth-stretching smiles, though his lips kept quivering and threatening to fall off his mouth. Gee, everybody was so nice. Everyone's halo was so golden. This was a really nice place, and Stone was glad he had found it. He had been looking so long.

As they walked along, Stone's eyes were drawn by the sound of barking, and he looked over to the left. Dogs, about two dozen of them held in pens just inside a barnlike structure. One dog looked familiar. As if it was buried somewhere in his mind. And as Stone focused, the dog, too, seemed to stare back at him, though it made no sound. The two mindless creatures stared hard for several seconds, and then Stone was dragged off. Funny, something about the dog made him— But the moment he began trying to remember where he had seen it, a splitting headache roared through his skull. So he stopped. And just let the golden haze drip back over everything.

The two led him about six blocks and then turned down a side street to a long log building.

"This is where all the new pods are brought," one of the gray robes said. "Here you will be shown the ways of the Perfect Order."

"Thank you," Stone said, grateful that they would be so kind as to give him anything. A worthless piece of garbage like him—Pod #47. Inside the place there were long rows of bunkbeds, about twenty on a side, for a total of nearly forty men in a room only about fifty feet long by twelve wide. So that when men on each side had their legs extended out, it was impossible to walk down the middle without going through a tangle of feet and toes.

"This is Pod number 47," the guards said as they walked Stone into the room. "Where is there a free bed?"

"Here," one of them spoke up, apparently the Group Leader, as he wore a gray robe while Stone and all the other new inductees, the lowest of the pecking order, wore brown.

"You will come here," the Group Leader leader said, taking Stone by the ear, squeezing hard and pulling him down the middle aisle all the way to the back. "The top bed is yours," he said, releasing Stone's ear. Stone stood in front of him, not moving, having a hard time focusing his eyes on one spot long enough to see anything. "You are Pod number 47. You will do nothing without being told to do it by me. I am Group Leader. You will not shit, sleep, or eat without command. Do you understand all this, Pod number 47?"

"Yes, Group Leader," Stone said, sorry that he had angered the Group Leader, though he did not quite know how he had done so. "I will do nothing without your permission."

"Now, climb up on your bed and sit there. Do not move," the Group Leader said as he turned and walked back up to the front of the room. Stone somehow dragged himself up the side of the bunk, where there was a small but rickety ladder. His hands and legs weren't working too well. The drugs, aside from affecting his brain, also didn't do wonders for his whole nervous and muscular system. Everything felt as if it was out of sync, like if he told his body to move his right hand it might just as easily twitch his left big toe. His signals, to say the least, were crossed up.

They sat there on the sides of their beds, their legs dangling over for nearly an hour, though none of them had much concept of time. Under the brainwashing and the constant stream of drugs into their bodies, time was nonexistent. For they had no pasts—or futures. Only the dreamy, fogenshrouded eternal now. After an indeterminate time, the Group Leader paraded up and down the rows cracking them each on the head with a long stick.

"Move, you worthless pods," he screamed as he smashed at them, though none could really feel all that much pain with all the junk in their bloodstreams. Still, like frightened dogs, they scurried along down the center aisle and out of the building. Stone was the last and took a good shot on the back of the head that he felt even through the golden haze. The Group Leader led them down a street, where they passed the late-afternoon workers coming in from the surrounding forests. A whole line of elephants, a dozen or more, were hauling forty-foot logs as the construction around the place continued. Somewhere inside Stone's rational self, a spark the size of a pinhead wondered where all the fucking elephants were coming from. But the question wasn't even acknowledged by the "cleansed" portion.

The Group Leader led them to a dining building where other cultees were already sitting, these all of higher ranks, with gray, even a few black, robes. The pods were all taken to one side of the long mess hall. Their section was screened off, as the highest ranks didn't like having to see the slobberings of the newest recruits. The Group Leader marched them around the table and then commanded them all to sit. They sat down, facing one another from a few feet across the table. Not a face showed any friendship, or fear. Nothing. They were like mirrors facing one another, each reflecting the other but offering nothing of its own.

Stone was staring into the face of a badly burned man whose vacuum eyes were trained right on Stone's nose. They looked at each other's noses for a good five minutes, Stone getting lost in the dripping nostrils. Suddenly there was a clanking sound, and metal cups were put out in front of them. These were quickly filled with Golden Nectar, which was poured from a large pitcher by the kitchen staff. The Group Leader ordered them to drink. And watched carefully, to make sure every drop was swallowed by every mouth.

Then they were allowed to eat. Other servants carried loads of gruel and watery soup around to their tables. Though few of them were hungry. But the Group Leader commanded them, "Eat!" And they did so, letting their arms drop, grabbing a piece of bread, dipping it mechanically in pasty gravy and then lifting it into their mouths. Their jaws chewed repetitively over and over without the slightest sense of taste or enjoyment. They ate because the Group Leader commanded them to. And he ordered them to because their bodies would die without sustenance. And the Guru needed their strong bodies for his holy works.

When they were done, they were led back to the barracks as the sunset died out to an inky blackness that suffused the sky. There were few lights around the place. The authorities didn't care whether their underlings smashed into things or not. Devotees were a lot more expendable than the fuel needed to maintain lights. The Group Leader led them back down the main street at a slow gait. He had lost two pods in the last week already. The dumb bastards had walked right into the sides of buildings, smashed their faces up so bad they were useless. Pods without the proper guidance were like chickens with their heads cut off.

He led them back into the bunkhouse and headed them back to the various beds like infants who didn't quite know where to go or what to do. Once they were all sitting on their mattresses, the Group Leader stood at the front of the log room and screamed out.

"Sleep!" He waited a few seconds, making sure they had heard. "Lie down," he bellowed again, and they all followed his orders. "Close your eyes." And like good and obedient children, they did close them. And lay there in stupors. Comas without dreams, cessation of activity without rest, sleep without peace.

SIXTEEN

When Stone awoke the next morning, someone was banging on his head, a voice was screaming into his ear. His eyes slowly opened, though they sure as hell didn't want to. He didn't feel like anything, didn't even feel human. Just a fuzzy dumb thing that followed the commands that were given it.

"Rise, rise, you worthless pods," the Group Leader yelled as he rushed around, smacking at all of them, forcing them from their beds so that some crashed out onto the wooden floor cracking things here and there.

"When a Group Leader commands you, you will obey at once! Do you hear me, pods?"

"Yes, Group Leader," they all answered back though some could hardly mumble the words, their mouths open with a constant stream of saliva coming out like an old alcoholic. One of the side effects of the large amounts of drugs in the Nectar was a problem with many of the bodily functions. Drooling, vomiting, pissing, shitting in pants and bed were not uncommon. Group Leader led them down the street to a circular wooden building about forty feet in diameter. Inside were other pods, already down on their knees as they prostrated themselves before the image of the Guru, with a huge rainbow aura behind him.

"Bow down on your knees, scum," the Group Leader screamed, kicking and smacking them as he led them to the altar, where candles were burning all around the six-foot-high portrait of Guru Yasgar behind glass.

"Thank you, oh Great Yasgar, for perfecting our imperfections," the Group Leader intoned.

"Oh, thank you, Great . . ." they all mumbled after him, their faces squashed down into the wooden floor.

"And though I am a worthless scum floating on a swamp . . ."

"I am worthless scum floating on . . ." Stone muttered vacantly after the rest of them.

"Still, I am grateful for the love that Guru Yasgar has shown for me."

"Gradeful for love that Yasgar has thrown me," Stone mumbled incoherently, letting his lips go slack as soon as he was done.

"Now rise, worms, and have your morning Nectar." As Stone rose up, he was handed a goblet from one of the robes who walked around dispensing the "cleansing" water. Again they drank it down under the watchful eyes of the Group Leader. Then they were all led outside again. They were taken along the main street, and as they came to different buildings the Group Leader would take some of the pods and direct them through the doors, where they would be put to work at different tasks. The Guru harnessed their abilities. That was, after all, their great "contribution" to the cult. Their work would enable Yasgar to expand his cult into the surrounding mountains, then the state, then . . .

All of them were left off at one place or another until the only one left was Stone and the Group Leader.

"Come with me, Pod number 47," the Group Leader said, whacking Stone along the shoulder with his stick. "You shall be given a most prestigious job—that of stirring the Golden Elixir." He led Stone for about five blocks, until they came to a windowless building with guards all around it. The place had the best security in the whole town. The Group Leader gave a signal to the guards and led Stone inside to a long warehouse-type setup with huge canisters, vials, powders all over the place with chemical names stamped in red letters on their sides. In the center of the floor were two immense stainless-steel vats a good ten feet high, perhaps six wide, with platforms built around their tops. And on one of the wooden platforms was a robed man, a gray robe, walking around the platform with a huge paddle dug into the vat, which he stirred.

"This, Pod number 47, is where the sacred Golden Nectar is made." Stone looked on dumbly as he saw an elophant appear from out of the shadows at the end and pick up a large black canister. It walked with the thing in its trunk up to the vat where the man was stirring, and holding it up, shook some of the green powder into the brew until its handler, riding on its back, kicked it on both ears twice and it stopped pouring, turned, and set the canister back down.

"You see, Pod number 47," the Group Leader said, leading Stone up the wooden stairs that led to the platform around the lip of the unmanned vat. "We keep this brewing operation going twenty-four hours a day. Or how would we supply the great need we have for the God-given liquid? You will work a twelve-hour shift, then be relieved. This is your new job, Pod number 47. You are fortunate indeed. It usually takes brownies, stage four, many months to attain this high station."

"I am a worthless worm," Stone began, though it wasn't he who spoke. Rather it was some drugged-out part of him that had taken possession of his mind and body. "I do not deserve such an honor, Group Leader."

"That is absolutely correct, Pod number 47," the Group Leader replied as he reached the top of the platform. He and Stone stepped onto it and looked down into the cauldron filled with thick liquid. "But the Guru has entrusted you with this job because he knows you can do it." Stone looked down into the boiling vat of gunk. It was yellowish, the consistency of tapioca pudding.

"Once the fires are turned on underneath," the Group Leader said, reaching down and igniting a jet that instantly lit a whole set of burners beneath the vat, "you must not stop stirring until the flame is turned off again—or someone relieves you here. Or the Nectar will burn. The sacred drink will burn. Do you understand what I'm telling you, Pod number 47, the seriousness of this job?"

"Yes, Group Leader," Stone replied, already feeling dizzy from the fumes arising from the vat.

"Now, all you must do is walk around the vat and stir with this paddle." He demonstrated, slowly moving around the platform as he dug the long aluminum canoe paddle deep into the drug mush so every bit of it was stirred around like a chef making stew for a giant.

"Now you try it, Pod number 47," he said after about twenty seconds.

Stone took the canoe paddle, and felt nervous. He was such a worthless piece of spit. He could not handle such an important job. It was too hard, too complicated for his mind to understand. But the loud crack of the Group Leader's stick right over the bridge of his nose, which sent a jolt of pain even through the drug fog, made Stone start walking. He held the canoe paddle hard because the stuff below was so thick that it kept threatening to suck the whole implement down. With the flames on, the cauldron of yellow gunk began to bubble quickly, and Stone could see what the Group Leader had meant about the stuff burning. For he had to stir faster and harder to keep it from coagulating on the bottom and along the sides. It was hard, straining his tired arms and brain to their limits.

The Group Leader stood behind him, following Stone around the platform like his shadow for about ten minutes as the liquid gradually changed from yellow to gold and grew thinner in texture. Stone's stirring and the heat broke up the various powders that were in it and evened the consistency. Suddenly, from above, on a wooden platform that Stone hadn't seen before, a foreman ran over and looked down into Stone's vat.

"That's it—you're cooked," he screamed out, motioning for Stone to turn down the flame. Stone looked confused, but the Group Leader showed him how to reach down and turn the gas knob to the left. It seemed like quantum physics to Stone's tortured mind. But he tried to learn it. He knew they were depending on him. It was a very important job.

With the gas jet down, the Group Leader motioned for Stone to step back. The elephant walked forward, around the front, and grabbed hold of the great vat. Placing its trunk over one edge, it pulled the whole thing over so it swiveled on huge bolts, and poured the mixture into a long trough, where it flowed away bubbling like lava from a volcano. The trough automatically fed the Nectar into rows of bottles all lined up with little funnels in their openings. The whole thing was very ingenious, allowing a few men and an elephant to make vast quantities of the stuff so that other pods could just come in and take the bottles off for the constant mouths that had to be fed.

"Good, Pod number 47. Now the elephant will refill the vat with the right proportion of chemicals," the Group Leader said as Stone watched the elephant pull the now-empty vat back upright so it locked into place on some catches. The huge beast headed back about fifty feet over to a wall, directed by the gray robe atop it. The trunk wrapped around a green barrel, and the elephant walked quickly back to the vat above which Stone stood. It emptied the powder in until the canister was empty, then went back for another.

"Now you must water it with this hose," the Group Leader said, showing Stone how to aim the stream down and get all the powder evenly wet. "The elephant will be adding dry powder; you must wet it enough to stir. And then just enough so it is the consistency of the Golden Nectar." It was all too much for Stone's brain. He felt a pounding headache surge through his skull. How could they expect him to remember all this? But he watched and then tried to imitate the Group Leader. He aimed the hose, though his hand shook. Everything shook from the drugs. It was hard.

He stepped out of the way as the elephant came back with a load—this time black chunks of stuff that had a sour smell.

"That is the opium," the Group Leader said. "Make sure

to break it up fine. Sometimes you must smash it with the paddle." Stone tried to do what the Group Leader said, lifting the paddle and forcing the chunks against the side of the vat. Yes, it worked. Even a useless worm like him could do something. Stone felt a surge of infantile pride surge through his zombie brain.

It took nearly ten minutes for the elephant to fill the vat up again. Under Group Leader's watchful eyes, Stone kept watering the gunk down until it looked about right. He reached down and turned the gas jets, and they sprang into flames below. Within minutes the huge vat was starting to puff and boil, and Stone had to move fast, walking around the cauldron with the long paddle dug deep into the drug soup. The Group Leader watched the whole operation two more times and then finally left, satisfied that the pod knew how to handle it.

For hours Stone stirred the stew of ten of the most powerful mind-altering drugs known to man. He had no idea in his 40-IQ-level brain what it was he was making. Just that it was important. The Guru was depending on him. And the Transformer, with his red eyes. So he concentrated all the mental power he could generate and walked around the vat, stirring for his life. For Stone had still a tiny speck of imagination somewhere within the "cleansed" brain. And that dark vision kept visualizing the elephant turning on him if he made even a single mistake. It would lift him high in its trunk, then dash him into the boiling chemicals. Even a zombie brain didn't want to go out like that.

SEVENTEEN

Stone was exhausted by the time he was relieved that night. He could hardly move a muscle. But at last the Group Leader came and collected him, and he joined the line of other pods. They were all marched back to the mess hall for more Golden Nectar before a hearty meal of unknown meat and overcooked dumplings. Every time Stone even vaguely started coming out of his trancelike state, they were right there with more of the potent brew. The Guru knew exactly how much to give his disciples—and then a little more, just to be on the safe side.

So by the time Stone actually got to eating, the drug was already in his bloodstream, and instead of eating gustily he just stared blankly down, like all the others, and took one slow forkful at a time, as if he could take or leave the slop set before him. When they were done, the Group Leader called them to their feet and marched them to the Temple of the Aura, where Stone had first been "initiated" into the cult.

When they walked inside, there were already a number of pods and gray robes around the floor. The Transformer himself sat in his robe on a great throne made of skulls in the center of the room. Even from across the floor, Stone could see those ruby eyes burning, and a shiver shot down his backbone. There is a fear even among the comatose. The

Group Leader led them to form a circle around the High Priest, joining in with several dozen others who had already started moving in a slow line.

Drums and rasping hornlike instruments sounded from the shadows, and the Group Leader motioned for them to bend down and pick up what was at their feet. Skulls. Stone shuddered inside and his hand twitched a little even as it followed the command. The thing had been dead for a while. It was mostly bone, though there were still clumps of flesh, a few matted little pieces of scalp still attached to the surface, as if the thing had been scraped but was not entirely clean of its former covering of flesh. Stone was far more terrified of the Transformer—or even the Group Leader— than the cold skull he held in his hands.

"Dance, dance around the High Priest," the Group Leader screamed, smacking at them with his stick. They began turning, holding the skulls out in front of them, waving them up and down. The drums grew faster, and suddenly they were all zooming around, and Stone felt dizzy and as if his legs were about to collapse under him. The High Priest stood up on his throne of shimmering ivory bones and exhorted them on. And under Stone's drugged gaze he seemed to grow, to rise into the air right above them until he was as tall as the ceiling itself. And again Stone didn't know what was real, what was not. The question didn't even have meaning. Just that he was in a world where he understood nothing and dumbly feared everything.

The dance seemed to become a tornado of motion until they were all whirling around the room, their robes spinning out wide and the drums pounding, their heads all twisting around as if there was thunder in their skulls. And just when Stone was sure he was going to fall down and smash his face into the floor, the Transformer suddenly screamed "stop" and held both of his long skeletal arms up. The dancing scores of pods came to a stop, though many of them collapsed immediately from the dizziness or kept going around like psychotic tops, smashing right into the walls, cracking their faces into bloody pies.

"First comes the holding of the skull," the Transformer intoned, his voice booming out over them making their very bones rattle. "Then comes the holding of the flesh." With the word *flesh*, dozens of women came streaming out of curtains on each side of the room. They were all young, beautiful, though none of the drugged men could particularly recognize the aesthetic charms of the young creatures. The unclothed women came running up to the pods, each one picking out her particular Love Pod. Instantly they were all over them, wrapping their arms, their legs around their chosen man. Kissing him, making cooing and aahing noises. A petite blonde not older than twenty and wearing nothing but bones over her breasts and loins wrapped herself to Stone like wallpaper to a wall and dragged him down to the ground. Stone didn't know what the hell was going on—but it was the High Priest's orders.

The woman stroked him and fondled him and groped him, and in spite of himself, in spite of not knowing where the hell he was, who he was, or what was going on, Pod #47 suddenly felt his pulse quickening and his manhood stiffening. And before he knew it, she was atop him and riding him as she writhed and made weird sounds. And though Stone's brain was in another dimension, his body was in *this* one. For the body is an animal. It doesn't need the brain around for it to take care of business.

EIGHTEEN

And so it went for days, perhaps weeks. Stone didn't even know time was passing. In the zombie mindset of his drug-induced trance, he was able to carry out basic functions—eat, sleep, shit—and perform his work at the drug plant, where he stirred the huge vat for long hours at a time, feeling himself grow even headier from the fumes that sometimes threatened to topple him over into the boiling muck. Not that he knew real fear under the Golden Nectar. Nor pleasure, nor pain. There was just obedience. Like ants carrying out their duties without question. Guru Yasgar had successfully turned men into an army of the living dead. And he had only begun.

Although Stone had no sense of mortality in his state, still he didn't want to fall into the great vat of drugs he paddled. But the fumes made it such hard going that he had to turn his head as he walked around the high wooden platform stirring. Had to turn away, trying to breathe in what little air there was coming from cracks in the wooden walls. The building had no aeration system, no safety features of any kind. The very thought was laughable. Men were expendable. Everything else was not. They were like light bulbs, used until they popped and then replaced.

On the fifth day of his tending to the drug pot, Stone

suddenly heard a scream in the late afternoon and glanced over toward the other vat and his fellow stirrer, just in time to see him slipping over the side of the steel cauldron—and right into the thing. His screams only lasted a second, and then he went under. Stone could see from his vantage point the man's hands waving wildly above the boiling mixture. Then it, too, went under, and within seconds the whole mess began boiling over.

"Emergency, emergency overflow," the foreman screamed as he rushed down from his overseeing station on an even higher platform above. He ran over to the boiling stew pot and slammed the Emergency Off switch on the gas jets beneath the pot. The flames went out—but the liquid didn't. The stuff cascaded right over the top of the great iron container, splashing down the sides—and over the foreman. He screamed as Stone watched, still walking around, for he knew if he stopped for even seconds his might go the same route. The stuff was hot as boiling tar and stuck all over the foreman's flesh and face like smoking napalm. He raced around the floor smashing into things as other supervisors yelled and ran around, the whole place had erupted into a mad chaos.

The Nectar-coated foreman, his whole body smoking from the superhot coating of a dozen different mind drugs, ran right into Stone's gas jets below, and his stomach hit against the steel side of the burner system. His face and chest folded over forward into the rows of flame, and he burst into fire himself, as the stuff in the state it was in was highly inflammable. Now he was on fire and screaming, a human torch rushing around the floor threatening to take the whole place down, as every square inch of it was made of wood.

"Burndown! Burndown!" the second foreman screamed out, rushing over past the burning torch of smoking flesh and turning off Stone's flames as well. Two other robed cultees came rushing over from across the floor and splashed buckets of water from the water tank that fed the drug mix. The burning man slammed facedown onto the floor, where he continued to writhe around like a snake on fire. The others splashed their ten-gallon buckets over the whole mess. And within seconds the fire was out. The flesh-bubbling dying thing on the floor mewed like a squashed kitten.

The operation was shut down for about an hour while the whole thing got sorted out. The body of the other stirrer was dragged out of the muck. He looked about as bad as the burned husk of foreman on the floor, his whole body blackened now with a charcoallike substance that coated him from hairless head to fleshless toe. Both bodies were put into a wheelbarrow, and Stone, while his pot was being emptied and cleaned, was told to take the load over to C building. The new foreman was going to take the time to clean out both cauldrons. Make sure there were no further problems. Guru Yasgar would make heads roll if there were. Or worse.

One of the slightly higher-ranking pods—a class-C pod as compared to Stone's own Pod D status—helped him with the foul-smelling barrow and guided them to the north side of town. Stone hadn't been in this section before, and he saw that it was empty of buildings after they had gone about four blocks. There was a large field, then a hill, and on the other side, a long two-story-high log structure. Only, this one looked more finely carpentered than many of the other buildings in the camp. The walls were sealed and tight, the roof without leaks.

Stone and Pod #83 came to the door, where two guards were armed with submachine guns, the only place in the town other than Yasgar's own palatial residence where there were armed men.

"Delivery of two terminated pods," said Pod #83, holding the right handle of the wheelbarrow.

"All right, bring them in," the guard replied in a bored manner, pushing back the door and pointing to the ramp to one side of the building. They walked over and, getting a good start as there was nearly five hundred pounds of human sludge in the barrow, rushed it up the ramp and inside. It smelled inside. Stone, even in his somnambulent mental state, noticed it instantly. Or rather, his nose did, which began twitching and snorting all on its own, so foul and distasteful was the odor. And in his dim-witted brain Stone knew as well what the smell was.

"Over here, over here," the guard said impatiently, pointing to a crude conveyer belt. It was about a yard wide and had foot-high walls of tin-covered slats on each side of it so nothing could pop up off of it. Which was a good idea, considering the kind of load Stone and Pod #83 were carrying. As they lifted the decomposing bodies, softened by the flame so that big slabs of them fell off, Stone and his helper swung the bodies up and onto the conveyer belt. Blood and slime and charred gunk splashed up onto the tin sides and some came up and got them in the face. Though neither man was noticing such things.

"Good, now back off," the guard said, as he motioned for the two to get out of the way. He walked over to a small gas-powered generator and pulled the cord on it hard. The engine didn't catch the first time, but on the second try it burped to life and gave out with a loud thumping sound. The conveyer belt began to move, and within Stone's mindlessness there was a ripple of curiosity. He hadn't even known these things still existed anymore.

The conveyer belt took the two still-smoking bodies down along the wooden canal about ten feet, where they disappeared inside a large metal box about ten feet long and six wide. There was a loud grinding sound from inside and then sounds of all kinds of things being snapped and crushed as the whole tin structure vibrated around on its supports. It only took about a minute, when the guard motioned them to walk to the other end and put the wheelbarrow under a round opening at the far end of the metal box. They placed the barrow right beneath the opening and the guard pulled a lever on the side. The round hole began extruding a ground-up burgerlike substance from its multiple holes. The bloody tendrils of human flesh poured out of the grinding machine and into the wheelbarrow. It only took about a minute for both corpses to be completely ground down into the same texture of chopped meat—bones, brains, eyeballs, fingernails, and all.

"That's it," the guard said, pulling the lever back and forth a few more times to force the last few worms of human flesh out of the grinding machine. "Take it to the commissary." Stone and Pod #83 turned and rolled the thing back out of the place and down the ramp, then walked slowly so as not to slop any of the nearly overflowing ground chuck onto the ground. And as they walked, Stone felt strange. It wasn't that he could really think all that clearly about the events of the last hour, but something didn't feel good inside. As if he had swallowed poison—in his brain.

But if the grinding operation made him feel strange, when they arrived at the back door of K building and several assistant chefs came to the door to let them in the back way, Stone suddenly found himself ready to puke. For they were in the kitchen. The side entrance to the main dining area for the whole village. The cooks led the way down a slop-encrusted, fly-buzzing hallway and then into a cooking room where big pots were cooking over fires everywhere. The smell of sour bread and rotting vegetables was thick in the air.

"Put them over here," one of the cooks said, indicating a long wooden trough that had been once used to feed pigs. The wheelbarrow was tilted to the side as they both pulled up hard the handles of the barrow and the load of freshly chopped meat was deposited into the trough. The cook leaned forward and scraped out all that was still stuck inside the wheelbarrow. And even as Stone and Pod #83 turned and started wheeling the empty barrow out of the kitchen, the cooks were already grabbing handfuls of the meat and cooking it up into big square loaves of meat loaf. Martin Stone, although he hadn't eaten for nearly twelve hours, and was most definitely not a gourmet even when not at the mental level of an amoeba with Alzheimer's disease, still didn't think he was going to have lunch today.

NINETEEN

Once the whole mess in the Nectar factory was straightened out, which took a good two hours, Stone was back at work slaving over a hot drug vat. He stirred and he tried to feel nothing. The drug was certainly pushing him in that direction, with enough chemical force to subdue ten men. But Stone wasn't an ordinary man. The Indians who had saved him had termed him the "Nadi," giver of death. Such men were endowed with strengths, willpowers, depths of grit that made them . . . different. Thus Stone, unlike any of the hundreds of others who had been put through the "aura cleansing" process—and hooked on the Golden Nectar—*felt* something.

It was his soul, his heart, that made him feel something. A spark of disgust, a germ of revulsion. A stirring in the guts that began fighting back against the blinding and deafening drugs. And as he walked around the platform, paddling the immense aluminum oar through the bubbling swamps of chemical brainfuck, Stone started growing angry. Within his idiocy he didn't even know he was angry, but felt a gnawing bite that grew to a burning rage. And Stone's face began loosening up a little from its dead, glazed expression, and his teeth began grinding together hard as he stirred.

He had been back about an hour and a half at the oar

when there was a big commotion at the front door and the guards were throwing themselves prostrate on the wooden floor. Stone gulped hard as he turned his head, continuing to walk the platform. It was—the Guru himself, the Great One. He had come to check out the damage to his precious drug-making equipment.

"Was there any damage to the vats themselves?" the Guru asked. It took all of Stone's nerve to even look at the man. He was huge, Stone could see that, even hidden within the all-encompassing black robe. His hood was thrown back, and Stone could see the round jowled face, the black eyes like black holes in space that could swallow whole planets, let alone men, the mouth with a twisted, amused smile that bespoke pain and blood—tons of it. His ears pricked up as Guru Yasgar walked around the place inspecting the damage.

"There can't be any more problems," he said with a raspy edge to his throat that set Stone's hair on end. The man hardly sounded as if he had been born on earth, or had sprung from the womb of a human woman. "Because within two days we begin our shipments out to the surrounding countryside, ship our Nectar out so that others may benefit from the attainment of Perfect Aurahood." The new foreman of the drug building nodded fervently as he walked along just paces behind Yasgar.

"Yes, Great One, no mistakes," the man said, knowing this was his chance to rise rapidly in the cult. "We have tested all gas jets and drainage systems. Everything is working perfectly." Stone suddenly sensed that the Guru was about to glance up at him, and he ripped his head away from looking down and walked zombie-faced around the platform like an ox.

"He is a good stirrer," the foreman said, noticing the Guru looking up. "And we have replaced the stupid pod who fell in with an experienced pod who had moved on to another job." He pointed up at the second vat, which had overflowed earlier. The stirrer was big, with a huge chest, which without shirt as he pushed hard was covered with a copper sheen of sweat.

The Guru surveyed the situation for a minute, taking in both men as he looked back and forth. Whatever he was looking for, he seemed satisfied.

"Good, good, all is proceeding according to plan," the hacksaw blade of a voice sawed out. "It shall soon be our destiny," he said, looking around at the other four men who were involved in keeping the fires going and the chemicals pouring into the vats, "to control this whole country. To spread our word, our way of doing things. Our message will be the world's message."

"The world's message," the others shouted back as one. They stood stiffly before him, ramrod straight, their eyes aimed ahead as no man dared look right into that dark, fat, swirling face, those pits of eyes that seemed to pierce anything like twin swords. The Guru suddenly turned with a swirl of his black robe and headed out the door. The Nectar makers looked at each other with terrified faces. They knew that they would wind up in C building if there was even the slightest mistake.

Thus, they allowed Stone to work just a ten-hour shift that day, as they didn't want to risk his being exhausted and adversely affecting their operation. The other man was released as well, and a new shift was put on. Stone was told to report back at eight in the morning, and he headed out, his head whirling from the day's violent events. Things were shaking up inside him, there was no question about it. An earthquake had gone off inside his brain, and the aftershocks were rippling along every fiber of his being.

That night was the weekly Ceremony of the Aura, where the Guru himself would perform the ritual. Stone marched in along with the rest after they had eaten dinner. He had eaten his vegetables—but had made sure they were served on a different plate than the meat. He would never eat meat in this place again. He didn't know much, but that much he knew.

The pods were gathered in a large circle around the Great

Room and then handed their goblets of Golden Nectar. Stone waited until the server had just walked past him, and, making a quick glance around, saw that no one's eyes were on him. He tilted his head back but lifted the long sleeve of his brown robe—and poured it right inside. The stuff was sticky and dripped down his armpit and chest. But he got away with it. He lowered the goblet, wiped his mouth, and smiled that dumb smile that they all got right after drinking it. He held the cup out with a dead stare so the server could take it back.

When they had all finished, they were commanded to begin dancing around the room as drums began welling up from hidden musicians around the room. The circle of drugged-out pods and higher robes started turning, slowly at first, like the wheel of a great wagon. But after a few minutes, as the drug really hit home and their bodies got loose like rag dolls and the music swelled, they moved faster. Skulls were handed to them by half-naked girls, and the dancing men grabbed them from the outstretched hands as they flew by, like brass rings from a merry-go-round. Holding the skulls, they waved their arms in the air dramatically, spinning them, making them part of their dance, bone batons.

Already Stone could feel something happening inside him. He hadn't had a dose of the Elixir for nearly sixteen hours now. And it was starting to wear off, slowly, for they had them all doped up to the near-limits of human tolerance. But enough so that his brain began clearing, a few of the cobwebs were brushed away, the doors over the rooms to his thoughts and memories began opening. And it hurt. The withdrawal began immediately. His muscles ached even as he danced and jumped along with the rest of them. He could feel a cold sweat break out over his entire body as the withdrawal began making the nervous and circulatory systems aware that something unpleasant was up.

Suddenly a cloud of smoke seemed to fill the entire center of the long wooden floor, and the pods let out gasps of blissed-out terror. And even as they twirled around, from out

of the blue smoke appeared the Guru in his ceremonial long
red satin robe that looked as if it had been taken from a
cardinal or something, and forcibly, as there were bullet
holes and bloodstains around where the heart was. Beside
him was a woman dressed all in black leather, wearing
spiked studs around her shoulders, waist, and head. And on
the other side of the Guru sat a dog, which had bizarre
markings painted all over its side in bloodred symbols. It
glared ahead, its own head frozen just like the dancing
pods'. And Stone knew instantly, as it slammed into his
brain like a safe falling from the top of the Empire State
Building, that it was his sister, April, and the damn dog—
his damn dog. The bastard had stolen everything that was
his. Even his fucking brain.

Yet Stone could feel within the migraine headache that
rippled through his dazed head from the shock that he was
starting to get some intelligence back. But if just being off
the stuff a few hours was any indication, he was in for some
bad times. For even as he danced around the Guru as blue
smoke swirled in great swelling puffs from the wind created
by the dancing pods who circled ever faster, Stone's whole
nervous system began twitching, shivers of exquisite pain
running through his fingers, elbows, wrists, neck, and
knees. All his joints ached as if he had a very bad flu. And
the rage that Stone felt was so powerful as he saw the murderous Yasgar with all that was precious to him that Stone
made himself dance even harder, jump even higher, so that
he didn't explode or go mad from the pain and confusion
and the burning hatred inside him.

"Think, think, you bastard," he screamed silently to himself, though his mind was having a little bit of trouble returning to its operating circuit boards. He knew he couldn't
do anything now—he had to keep dancing and act as if
nothing was wrong. The machete-clutching guards who surrounded the room at least three on each wall were ample
proof of what would happen to anyone who even tried to
harm a hair on the Sacred One's head. So Stone danced and
made his twitching lips smile and laugh as the others were.

As if they were all in paradise when in fact they were all in hell.

The Guru waved his hands. "Faster, faster," he exhorted the pods. "Move, you slime. I command you. Make the skulls in your hands blurs. Thus the auras of the living and the dead are united." He held his hands to the ceiling sky and blue lightning seemed to slash down from above and right into his fingertips. And as Stone watched in growing horror and pain, he saw April, in her black leather Dominatrix outfit, pull out a whip and begin snapping it out at the twirling dancers. She smiled the smile of the demonically possessed as she cracked the whip, the long leather tongue taking pieces right out of cheeks and arms, slicing through robes here and there. But the pods only danced into more of a tornado fury.

On the other side of the Guru the damn dog joined in too, looking like some kind of creature from the mists of the Neanderthal days with its archaic symbols scrawled over it in red. It snarled at the dancers as they passed, reminding them to keep their fucking asses high, and their feet aslapping. And they did. And didn't need any more encouragement than those three and ten thousand milligrams of Nectar circulating through them.

They twirled for hours, screaming and dropping to the floor in writhing convulsions as many of their nervous systems overloaded completely and began short-circuiting. And as the hours went by, Stone felt things go from bad to worse. For he was coming off the stuff fast. Every cell in him was aching. His head was just a throbbing mess of gristle, his eyes watery and puffed out, hardly able to see. As he spun, tears sprinkled down—to see what had happened to the only two creatures he cared about on this entire fucked-up planet. The Guru had molded them both to his personal designer taste. Had added them to his entourage befitting the rule of a small but growing empire of the brainless. Even the fucking dog didn't have the spark it usually carried in its almond eyes. Stone tried to catch either of their eyes as he spun around them, knowing it was dangerous but having to try. To see if there was anything there at all anymore. He could see nothing. Though both of their gazes caught him at some point over the endless circlings, not a sign of recognition crossed their faces.

The ritual went on for hours, until the room was filled with the odor of sweat and the strong-smelling Nectar. But at last, about midnight, the Guru suddenly departed again, along with Stone's ex-family, in a swirling cloud of blue smoke. The pods left or were rolled out the door and back to the bunkhouses for the night. Now that he had stopped dancing, Stone's body was already starting to tighten up. He walked as if on razor blades—for his feet felt as if they were on fire—back to his barracks and slid into bed. There he lay, shaking and sweating, his teeth chattering together like marambas in a salsa band.

And through the cold night, as he wondered if he were going to live or die—and wouldn't at all have minded the latter—Stone discovered what all addicts had had to learn through the course of mankind's long addictive relationship with drugs. That what feels good when you first take it feels like the tortures of hell itself when you try to get off it. Stone was just a junkie with a monkey as big as a mountain gorilla climbing on his back, screaming out for more.

TWENTY

Stone couldn't have gotten more than a couple of hours of tortured sleep before he was awakened by the Group Leader, who did his usual screaming and stick-smacking number to get them all going. He felt like shit. Shit wasn't the word. He would have been happy to feel like shit. The gorilla on his back wasn't giving up. If anything, it was growing, its ugly paws ripping at his brain. Stone wanted some of the Golden Nectar. He could feel it inside. He craved it. His body was demanding, begging, pleading, cajoling him for it. But Stone just gritted his teeth and let the sweat pour down his face.

Fuck it. The pain was good. It hurt—but it cleared his mind. It razored through the curtain of fog that he had been in for the last week or more. It sliced through the cottony brain cells, screaming out reality to him. And Stone savored it. Let it rip into him. He would use the withdrawal to bring himself out of the drug stupor, would turn the pain into anger, and would direct it against the bastards who had done all this to him, to April, and to the damn dog. And to all the poor pods here, and those who had already died. Even as Stone made his face look blank, which was the hardest thing of all considering the amount of torment his mind and flesh were in, he rose from the bed, dressed, and joined the others, who were filing silently out, their eyes straight ahead, focused on infinity.

Stone managed to do the same thing at the morning Aura Ceremony—having slipped his Nectar down his sleeve. Though it smelled wonderful and his cells cried out for him to drink it—just a drop or two—Stone poured the fucking stuff down his robe, getting it all even stickier and fouler inside. But even that was just another irritant that he could use to drag himself from the shell of nothingness he had been nearly digested into. At the drug factory he walked in stiff-legged, mounted his platform, and began stirring. No one noticed a thing. No foremen or guards at the door noticed that beneath the blank expression, the eyes staring straight ahead, Stone was in fact seething. There was pain in those eyes, and rage in those lips, threatening to scream out at any moment.

But he didn't scream—he just walked and stirred. And when he felt the fumes from the drug start getting to him, Stone ripped off a few small pieces of material from the sleeve of his robe while he kept stirring, and put them in each nostril so he to some extent was able to keep the mind-altering fumes out. As he stirred throughout the afternoon, Stone saw them pouring vat after vat into large barrels and then stacking them at the far end of the factory. Already there were over a hundred of the barrels—and Stone knew they were heading out of there soon. Once the bastards started getting their slimy fingers onto the rest of Colorado, it would be all over.

Through the long painful day, Stone tried desperately to think up a plan—any plan. Hard enough under the best of circumstances, considering how outnumbered he was. But even harder in his present mental and physical state. Sweat poured down from every pore in his epidermis, and he was thankful for the long enclosing brown robe that hid his shaking from view. His suffering was his own. It was a private affair.

The Guru came in again late that evening just before the end of Stone's shift and he looked over the rising piles of barrels all filled to overflow with the Nectar. He seemed pleased with it all—and in a positively good mood for a Guru who most of the time emulated Adolf Hitler for all his demonstrativeness. The fat face smiled and his voice had an almost happy quality to it. At last his dark plans were coming to fruition. After a lifetime of crime and thievery, he was coming into his own. Would take his place alongside the great rulers of history. Only, *his* rule would last—unlike all the others', the Napoleons, the Caesars, the Hitlers and Mussolinis—for many, many years. They were mere bureaucrats compared to him. For he had a magic helper that none of them did—the Golden Nectar.

"The wagons will be here first thing in the morning," Guru Yasgar told the foremen, patting the barrels as if they were the thighs of his harem. "No problems."

"No problems, Great One," all the men cried out, throwing themselves into scraping bows before him as he left the place with a growl emerging from his whipping robe. Stone knew he had to act—tonight. After tomorrow it would be too late. That didn't give him a hell of a lot of time to get it together. And considering the fact that he appeared to be entering the main stage of his withdrawal process as he started puking his guts out into the Nectar, it looked even worse. Stone managed to guide the upchuck slop right into the drug stew and stirred it quickly in. No one noticed. Stone figured people who ate human burgers wouldn't mind a little puke in their drug malteds.

By the time he was sent off from his shift, he was a wreck and could hardly twitch and lurch his way out the door. The guards gave him the once-over, but lots of the stirrers could be seen going into similar physical contortions. The fumes were powerful. The turnover rate at the drug factory was extremely high. And those who left didn't usually get promoted upstairs—they croaked. It wasn't the kind of career those looking for a long-term situation would be happy in. But then, Stone wasn't planning on sticking around. He was getting out of this wretched place alive—or dead.

He staggered back to his bunk; most of the pods were already asleep. Group Leader whacked at him, driving him down the middle aisle into bed.

"To sleep, Pod number 47, to sleep! You must awaken at five o'clock. Nectar production has been stepped up."

"Great," Stone mumbled as he climbed up into his top bunk and fell down onto the hard bed.

"What was that, Pod number 47?" Group Leader asked him, leaning back and looking a little more closely at the man. Pods didn't usually answer back with smartass cracks.

"I said . . . thanks for telling me now," Stone said, talking in a slow monotone the way they all did. "It is an honor to produce more Golden Nectar for the Guru—for such a worthless being like myself to be of such service. I will sleep well tonight. Of that I am sure."

"Excellent attitude, Pod number 47," the Group Leader said with a grim smile. "I will note that on your performance chart. Perhaps someday you shall rise to gray robe."

"I am not worthy, Group Leader." Stone sighed deeply.

"No, you are not," the pod crew chief replied as he walked away toward his single up by the door to keep his eye on everything.

"Asshole," Stone couldn't help but mutter under his breath, which was better than jumping up and slugging the guy. But thank God the Group Leader didn't hear him. He lay there, letting the tension and the pain ooze from his body. Only problem was, it didn't ooze away as much as just keep bubbling up until he felt as if he was going to explode. The worst thing about the withdrawal, aside from the fact that he kept having to run to the shithole in the back of the place and let out with huge streams of diarrhea, was that it made his brain feel as if it was splitting into about a thousand pieces. But with ever-deeper descent into the torments of the drug-addicted flesh, Stone felt his mind growing clearer—and angrier.

He lay there and thought and thought. And when he had put it all off as long as he possibly could, gauging that it was about three in the morning and that he didn't have a hell of a lot of time, he at last sat up and said a silent prayer to whatever gods might be, and crossed himself unconsciously to ward off all the supernatural powers of the Guru. For though Stone was coming back to his old mind, he still feared Guru Yasgar, and the Transformer with that dead face, the glowing red eyes. How could the man even be human? There was more to this whole stinking ball game than he could yet understand. But then, he wasn't here to unravel the fucking mysteries of the universe—just to grab April and the flea-bitten dog—and get the hell out of there. Only, he had to do something first.

He rose, tried to plant his feet firmly on the floor as everything was spinning around, almost making him puke again. Stone walked slowly down the center aisle hoping he could even still fight. He wasn't sure things worked quite like they once did. But he was about to find out.

"Where the hell are you going, Pod number 47?" the Group Leader barked out as Stone came even with his bunk, where the man was half dozing with one eye open, his long stick held in his arms over his chest.

"I'm going to go knock the Guru's balls off," Stone whispered in the half-darkness. He couldn't help but let a smirk flash across his face. It felt good—even within the pain. Made it all worthwhile, in a way, that little smile. The Group Leader shot up from his bed like a cougar with a pinecone up its ass and came at Stone with the stick, ready to take his head off. As the stick flew in toward his skull, Stone slipped under it and slammed his fist up into the Group Leader's lower abdomen. With his index finger arched forward at midjoint, the pointed fist slammed into the man's guts and knocked all air out of him like bellows closing. The stick flew from his hand, and Stone caught it in midair and then guided the bent-over man who was making strange sounds below him around and out of the room—into a small utility closet off to the side where they could have a little discussion about a few things. Stone pushed the man right into the five-by-five-foot closet and closed the door behind him.

Just as the Group Leader starting rising up again, Stone
let him have a knee to the face. Various cracking sounds
resulted and a gush of blood instantly covered the man's
features. Stone needed information—and fast. He was going
to have to put the fear of God into this son of a bitch to make
him spill. Had to make the man more afraid of Martin Stone
than of Guru Yasgar. "Now you're going to tell me a few
things," Stone said after he had waited a few seconds,
enough time for the man's brain to at least be hearing things
again. "And you're going to tell me, because the way I figure it, you're an upper-echelon Group Leader and must be
on smaller doses of the Nectar. Otherwise, you wouldn't be
able to run things as efficiently. That means you can also
feel more pain."

Just as the man's eyes looked up to see if there was some
way he could attack, Stone slipped his hand down under the
Group Leader's ear and, just at the top of the neck and
pressing in his finger, gave a shiatsu push to the nerve. The
man started to scream, but Stone slammed his hand over the
gasping mouth. He didn't need any more visitors right now.
The acupuncture, meridian 12 point. His father had showed
him it—one of many places on the body where one could
inflict pain, paralyze, or kill. And from the looks of the
tortured face beneath him, Stone figured he was doing something right.

"Now—I won't hurt you again if you answer my ques-
tions, okay?" The Group Leader shook his head fast a few
times as Stone let up on the pressure and took his hand from
the man's mouth. He kept the finger just touching the skin,
ready to jam it in.

"Where are my weapons . . . my clothes?"

"I don't—" the Group Leader began. But Stone slammed
the index finger in like a spear and the man gasped as if the
devil had just pushed a pitchfork through his heart.

"Let's tell the truth, okay, asshole?" Stone said, almost
enjoying making the little bastard squirm after all they had
put him through.

"In—in building R—south side of town. All confiscated stuff is taken there."

"And second," Stone said with a deathly darkness in his face. "Where are the girl—the Guru's new woman—and the dog. Where are they?" The man looked as if he didn't want to answer that one at all. But Stone pressed again, and he spat out the words as though they were bullets.

"In the Royal Temple. The Guru has taken her as his Heavenly Wife—and they are to be wed in a few days."

"Great," Stone said, slamming the stick down hard on the side of the Group Leader's skull. The man collapsed in a heap on the floor. He'd be out long enough for Stone to get his thing done. And after that, it didn't really matter. He'd be out of there—or he'd be dead.

He made his way through the back alleys and streets until he reached the building the Group Leader had mentioned. Stone reconnoitered the place, making two complete circumferences before heading in. It was big—warehouse-size. Only trouble was, there was only one door that Stone could see—and it had a guard in front of it armed with an SMG. Stone wasn't in the mood to start cat-burglaring it up the side of the damn thing— coming down from the roof. No, this was all going to have to be out front, every bloody bit of it.

He walked suddenly from out of the shadows and straight toward the guard, waving at him to completely confuse the bastard. Stone came up fast on the man with one of the big artificial smiles that all the pods wore. "Group Leader just sent me to tell you this—" Stone said as he slammed his elbow around right into the guard's face. Once, twice, three times he cracked the elbow around into the center of the head. When he stopped, the bloody tangle of broken bone and blood was not quite the same man it had been a minute before. He pushed the guard backward and they both half tumbled through the door, the guard falling backward, where he began writhing around silently as he stroked his bloody face as if it was a baby.

Stone, seeing that the asshole wasn't any more trouble to him, grabbed the SMG and a bag of ammo the guy wore on his hip and instantly felt a whole lot better. With a little firepower maybe he could actually wreak some havoc around the place. Suddenly the odds seemed a lot less formidable than they had just seconds before. He made a quick visual scan of the place, swinging a small oil lamp that had been sitting by the door. The numbers of rows of shelves that ran off in every direction made it seem like an impossible task. But once Stone began walking around he saw that things were all logically broken up into categories—of clothes, boots, weapons, whatever. It didn't take all that long for him to find his stuff. He took off the filthy robe, coated on the inside from stem to stern with the Golden Nectar, and slipped into his black turtleneck sweater, motorcycle jacket, jeans, and boots.

That felt better. And better yet when he found his Ruger .44 and strapped the holster around his chest. Then the Beretta 9mm autopistol. And they'd laid the silencer down right next to it—how nice. Stone screwed it on, slammed a thirty-shot mag into the bottom of the thing, grabbing the ammo sack as well, and turned around. Now he was starting to get somewhere.

TWENTY-ONE

Stone headed through the darkness, toward the drug factory. There was no one out. That was one of the good things about a cult—they obeyed orders. Guards were posted here and there, but they were mostly set on the outer edges of the town to guard against invasion from the outside world. Somehow they hadn't really thought too much about attack from within. For those who went mad just fell down and began spasming, or else never got up from their beds one morning, dead in their sleep, unable to face another day. But no pod had ever struck back against the cult. Until now.

The withdrawal was still hitting Stone hard as ever. But he had already gotten used to it in a weird way, and just used the pain—the splitting headache—to drive himself on, the way a good boxer uses the blows he takes to wake him up and get his fighting juices flowing. Stone's fighting juices were sure as hell flowing. He was ready to take on the world. He moved low in the shadows, savoring his returning memory, his abilities slowly restoring themselves. It was as if he were being reborn.

He reached the drug factory and, looking up at the sky, saw that it was just at the edge of starting to change color from black to bruised purple. That meant dawn was coming in fast, like a fucking violet-hued freight train. And with it would come the carriers of the plague to the surrounding territories. He had to move now. . . . Oil lamps were burning inside the factory and Stone could hear the sounds of heavy work inside. The night shift. There would be at least four workers, two overseers, a guard or two. So he was dealing with a minimum of eight, a maximum of— He didn't know. There could be fifty fucking people in there for all he knew. But it hardly mattered—he had to go in and take the whole fucking place out. He wasn't going to allow a murderous scumbag like Yasgar to take over what pitiful remnants of America were left. There would be no chance of ever returning to some kind of real "civilization" then.

Stone took out both pistols, the big .44 and the 9mm, and walked out of the shadows and toward the front door. The guard on duty didn't even really take much heed of Stone when he saw him. People had been coming and going all night. But when he spotted the two rods in the pod's hands, the cult guard's whole face seemed to freeze up, even through his drug haze. Pods didn't have guns. And in the split second it took for him to realize what that meant, it was too late. The fast lived, the slow died. Even as he raised his rifle and reached frantically for the trigger, Stone's silenced 9mm spoke softly. But it spat out a burst of slugs that sliced into the man's chest and sent him flying backward, up the ramp and then crashing through the door that led into the Golden Nectar brewery.

There were seven men inside, the eighth was dying in a bloody pile on the floor. And they sure looked surprised to see one Pod #47 holding two nasty-looking firearms. Stone came tearing into the room, or at least what passed for tearing, on legs that felt as if they belonged to a ninety-year-old arthritic. Everybody was frozen—except for the stirrers atop the two steaming drug vats. They knew they couldn't stop —not for a second.

"Now, I don't want to hurt no one," Stone snarled as his eyes snapped back and forth around the room making sure no one tried anything dumb. "Just get out of here right now, and you can all live."

"Pod number 47, drop those guns immediately and return to your barracks," one of the foremen screamed at Stone, standing about ten feet away with one of the long smacking sticks in his hand.

"No chance, pal." Stone smirked back with a certain dark satisfaction that he didn't have to listen to these jerkoffs anymore, didn't have to follow their every command while his brain sat in the mud at the bottom of the ocean. The foreman, perhaps fearing the wrath of Yasgar should he let anything get fucked up, suddenly charged forward, raising the stick over his head as if he was going to behead Stone. But that wasn't quite how it worked out. For even as the cult officer got within a yard and started to bring the stick down, Stone's 9mm burped out another stream of bullets. They sliced the guy's whole face into Swiss cheese, with blood running out of the holes. The stick flew from his hands as he went flying backward, as though he had been kicked by a mule. His face red with blood that poured out onto his robe, the foreman slammed into one of the barrel stackers and they both went sprawling.

"Now, out. I mean it—right now!" Stone screamed out, letting another few shots go up into the beamed wooden ceiling, which sent a shower of dust and sawdust down over them all. But the two jerking dying things on the floor appeared to be enough even for the brain-cleansed. And they walked backward out of the building, their arms held high, their zombie faces showing traces of human terror. The stirrers kept going, though, torn between leaving and their posts—since they knew they were dead men if they budged.

"Down—and out," Stone shouted again, letting a stream of bullets dance across the sides of both vats.

"But it will all go up in flames," one of them protested.

"That's the general idea," Stone yelled back. "Now, down! I'm losing patience." He released another few rounds, even closer to them. The sound of bullets whistling by their skulls made the two let the paddles go and come tearing down the stairs. Stone kept his eyes firmly on them as they headed out the door; then he bolted it behind them.

Now he was alone. Just him, two corpses, and thousands of gallons of mindfuck juice. Well, they were all about to have a nice little party.

Stone slammed both pistols back into their holsters and rushed over to the controls in front of the gas jets. He turned both burners all the way up so their flames were a good five feet high and began reaching up around the sides of the vats. Then Stone turned the valves that released the precious poison by turning a huge tap on one side. The stuff poured down onto the floor, quickly inundating the jerking dead men, as if they were taking a final bath before an extended stay in hell. Stone rushed to the back of the place, where the rows of filled barrels stood waiting to head out into the world. Only, he wasn't going to give them the chance. He ran up and down the rows opening the spigots on the sides of the barrels. Their contents began pouring out onto the floor like a party of drunks who couldn't hold their liquor.

Suddenly he heard a crackling sound behind him and turned. The stuff had caught on fire over near the vats. The drug liquid that had poured out on the floor was a flaming sheet and reaching up toward the main vats. Stone knew what would happen when full contact occurred. Party was over. Time for the fat lady to sing. He tore ass down the center of the place, stumbling and almost going over like some Bowery drunk. The withdrawal was doing wonders for his whole balance system. But fire is a strong motivator. And already the entire side of the floor holding the vats was ablaze in a carpet of reaching yellow and red. Stone ran straight for the door, nearly slipping as he hurdled the two corpses on the floor, their blood spreading out for yards in each direction, mixing with the Golden Nectar, which nearly covered the entire wooden floor.

Stone could feel the flames reaching for him, singeing the hair on his head, making the whole left side of his body feel as if it was about a thousand degrees hotter than the right side. He reached the door, threw the bolt, and ripped the thing open. Stone knew there would be trouble waiting outside. But he'd worry about that in a second. The fire was burning his tail right now. He came tearing out of the place like a racehorse at the Kentucky Derby. And bowled right through about ten pods who were standing in front with sticks in their hands, apparently trying to get up the nerve to make a charge. Only, Stone came flying through them so fast they didn't have a chance to strike at him. By the time they turned and started toward Pod #47, who was still tearing ass away from the building, it was too late.

There was a sudden roaring sound from within the Nectar factory. And they could all see that the fire had grown a thousandfold. For the orange glow was streaming through every crack in the place, through the open door, through air vents in the roof. But that only lasted for an instant. Then came the explosion. It was an oddly peaceful explosion—in a way. Less sound than one might think—but incredible fury. For as the entire load of highly inflammable Nectar caught and released its great stored-up energy all at once, the burning blast rushed out in all directions. The log building that housed the factory had been well made, securely constructed. Strong enough to withstand the howling winds of winter. But not an explosion in its very guts.

Even as Stone continued to tear butt, getting to about sixty yards away, he heard the sound behind him. It was like being inside a thundercloud when it released its heavenly lion's roar. And then he didn't know what the hell was going on except that the whole world was bright yellow and he was being lifted and tossed around like a leaf with a firecracker tied to its tail. He literally flew right through the smoking air a good twenty feet up, and he suddenly knew how it felt to be a meteor entering the earth's atmosphere. Then he hit— and hard. Only his years of training and his still-youthful agility allowed him to come down without breaking anything. Though it hurt like hell.

The heat wave followed the blast itself, and he felt a rush of fifty-mile-per-hour superheated wind rush right over his back as if he was lying in front of a blast furnace. Then there was terrible screaming. And when he lifted his head after a few seconds and dizzily focused on the scene behind him, he

saw why. The pods who had been waiting to ambush him
were all human torches now. Every part of them burning as
if they were trying to light up the heavens all the way to
Alpha Centauri. Behind them the entire drug factory was
ablaze in a solid wall of flame. Nothing could be seen but
fire, already twisted beyond recognition from what it had
been just seconds before. The flaming pods ran wildly in all
directions, like moths caught in a campfire. Then they collapsed onto the ground, where they joined in the blaze.

Stone watched the conflagration for a few seconds. He
didn't feel good about seeing men die like that. But he did
feel a deep satisfaction that, whatever happened now, he had
put the expansion plans of the Guru—maybe even the exis-
tence of the cult itself—in big doubt. That was pretty good
for a man who could hardly walk and felt as if he had a
hangover from a thousand-year drinking bout. But his feelings of self-congratulations didn't last long. For as Stone sat
up, he heard sounds behind him from out of the flame-splat-
tered darkness. And as three figures came into view, Stone
knew he'd just gone from the fire into something much
worse. For coming at him with vengeance in their respective
eyes were Guru Yasgar, seated atop a raging tusked elephant, and Excaliber, the fucking traitor, who ran alongside
the rampaging giant as though he wanted the first piece of
the flesh pie of Martin Stone.

TWENTY-TWO

Having an elephant, tusks and all, with huge trunk waving in the purple dawn, coming straight at him, was not something Stone had ever experienced before. And doubtless he never would again. In fact, it didn't look as if he was going to experience much of anything after about the next five seconds. But even as he somehow made himself rise to both legs, which trembled like toothpicks riddled with termites beneath him, and pulled out both pistols into his hands, the Guru screamed out orders to the elephant and kicked it hard on both ears so the thing came to a skidding stop not ten feet from Stone. Yasgar screamed down something in a language that wasn't English to the dog, and it stopped as well. Stone had to admit, even in the midst of all the blood and death, that it pissed him off to see the dog obey a command so quickly and totally when he hadn't been able to get it to even fetch a fucking ball on command in the months they had been traveling together. And even as he thought it, he knew how absurd it was to be thinking about something so trivial when he was about to be squashed.

Guru Yasgar looked down at him from atop the immense beast of burden. He didn't look too happy about it all as the light danced over his face. Even off the drugs now, Stone had to admit it gave his heart a little bit of a turn to look up into that face. The man exerted an almost palpable power, the presence of evil as he stood up high on the elephant silhouetted by the violet dawn that slowly brightened the heavens behind him.

"Pod number 47—why have you done this?" the Guru asked. He seemed genuinely curious within his fury. It was something that shouldn't have happened, couldn't have happened.

"The name's Stone," Stone replied, looking up at the man high above him. "Pod number 47 died last night while I puked my guts out getting off this shit you addicted me to."

"It's impossible for any man to break free of a successful cleansing," Yasgar said as the elephant stared hard at Stone, as if it was praying it got the chance to squish his head like a rotten pumpkin. The dog, too, Stone saw with disgust, was giving him the once-over, its lips pulled back, its teeth showing. It was pointing at him, lining up tail, back, and nose to make a perfect line. Stone knew what that meant. He had only seconds.

"Well, sorry to disappoint you, Mr. Yasgar, but I did it. Don't you think so?" Stone nodded his head toward the burning drug factory behind him and let a smile play across his lips.

"I was going to have my elephant here, Shiva, rip your balls off, impale you on her tusks," the Guru said, letting his own smile flicker on the thick lips within the hooded robe. "But now . . . now I think that I will have your own dog kill you. Yes, that will be a fitting punishment for such terrible deeds." Yasgar looked down at the pit bull and again screamed out something that sounded to Stone like Greek, but was in fact demonic Sumerian incantations that the Guru used in many of his ceremonies taken from real scrolls, thousands of years old.

"*Nis Isshtar. Nis isshtar,*" he commanded the pit bull. Stone didn't know the exact meaning of the words, but he knew what they basically meant: rip out Stone's brains, heart, and lungs—and then hurt him. The dog growled and crouched low, the stance it took when it was about to leap on something's bones. Stone had seen the animal do it enough fucking times—only, it had always been on someone else. The very thought that the pit bull, after all they'd been through, was working for the other side, brought a little flush of moisture to Stone's eyes. He didn't mind dying. But going out with such a cloud of betrayal over the whole thing, that hurt, it really hurt. Perhaps, in its own way, more than anything. Even more than the pains of the withdrawal that continued to stream through his body.

Stone raised the Ruger toward the pit bull, knowing the 9mm wouldn't be enough. His hand closed hard around the butt and his finger reached for the trigger. But he couldn't pull it—even though he knew that if he didn't, it would be too late. Once the dog was airborne, he wouldn't be able to stop it even with a whole chest full of slugs. The animal seemed to suddenly go crazy. It twitched and foamed and jumped around as if it had Mexican beans up its ass. It was clearly having a problem carrying out the Guru's orders. Its jaws opened and closed, the razor-sharp teeth snapping down as if it was chewing some invisible enemy.

"Isshtar, Isshtar!" Yasgar screamed over and over, now standing to his full height atop the elephant so that he looked quite fearsome, even to the animal. But if the Guru expected that to take care of it, he was suddenly horribly surprised. For the dog just stood there, shaking harder, as if it was having an epileptic fit. It couldn't do it.

"All right, then," Yasgar screamed, with the full orange dawn now flaming behind him, making it look as though God was doing the lighting for the bastard. "I'll do it myself. Crush him," he commanded the elephant, kicking it on each side of the head with his spurred boots. "Crush him, smash his fucking brains out." Stone heard the Guru's voice slip out of its dark modulated tones into a gruff New York accent, and he could see the bastard's real roots in a flash. Not that it mattered.

For suddenly the elephant was coming forward, straight at him, with fury in its soup-bowl-size eyes. Stone fired right into the animal's chest and neck. But it was a joke.

Even a .44 wasn't stopping this sucker. Suddenly the beast
was there, towering above him like a mountain as its huge
gray trunk came slapping down at him. The first hit knocked
Stone to the ground as if he had been struck with a tree. And
even as he lay there dazed, searching for his pistols that had
fallen to the ground, the trunk came down a second time.
The elephant wrapped the long snout around Stone and lifted
him up into the air. It waved him around a few times as
though he was a baton for an orchestra of death, and then
held him far out about eight feet above the ground. Stone
looked back and could see the huge tusks of the beast pointing toward him. There was no question about what the elephant had planned for him next. It was shish-ke-Stone time.

But even as the beast let out a great trumpeting roar and
Yasgar raised his hands to the sky in triumph, wanting to see
the body ripped to shreds on the ivory spears, Excaliber
sprang up from the ground as though he had been fired from
a launching pad. The jaws opened to full width as he arced
right up into the air straight at the great beast. Then the pit
bull made contact with the trunk just above where it was
holding Stone. The jaws closed like a bear trap snapping
shut on a grizzly. And the elephant let out a trumpet that
woke the entire camp—even savages miles off in the mountains. The neighborhood was jumping this early morning.

The pit bull crunched hard again—and the trunk tore
cleanly in two, severed clear through by the guillotine jaws.
Stone found himself falling through the air with the trunk
still wrapped around him. Then everything was in a weird
kind of slow motion. He felt himself falling, falling through
the air as if forever, as the dog fell away in a different direction, its face covered in red. Then the elephant was up on its
hind legs as its trunk, only about a third its previous size,
spewed out gallons of blood like a hose gone mad. The red
ocean covered Stone as if it was raining down from the very
heavens.

And as it reared, the huge beast sent Yasgar flying off its
back. He fell a good twelve feet down the side of the thing,

landing on his back. And though Stone could see that the fall had by no means done him in, the same couldn't be said when the elephant came crashing down on him. Even as Yasgar started to rise from the dirt and reached inside his robe for a poison-tipped blade to take out Stone himself, the elephant gave off a throaty gurgle. Cutting off an elephant's trunk is like cutting off a man's cock—the damage to the beast's nervous system was too great for it to go on.

The many tons of gray hide came slamming right down on top of the Guru. And all his great powers of persuasion and mind control, his abilities to take over men's minds and women's bodies, was for naught. For he was squashed into a bloody pie beneath the beast. Stone saw the body disappear beneath the immense bulk of the dying beast and then a flood of blood, forced out under pressure, come shooting out from under the elephant. The tusked creature flopped once as if an electric current had gone through it and then it lay there motionless, the river of blood pouring from the hacked-off trunk as if someone had left the valve on in the family washing machine.

TWENTY-THREE

Stone looked at the dog. The dog looked at Stone. And they both got strange expressions on their faces. Then the dog got a real sheepish look and walked the twenty feet or so to Stone, where he rubbed up against his leg. Stone was touched by the gesture. The dog was obviously still having some brain problems himself, under the drugs and hypnotic commands of the Guru, but still he tried to show that things were okay.

"Don't worry about it, boy," Stone said, reaching down and scratching the blood-soaked canine behind the ears. "We've all been doing some things we didn't like lately. And anyway, you didn't attack me, right?" For which fact Stone would be forever grateful. And from the looks of the puddle that seeped out from beneath the quivering elephant, it didn't look as if the Guru was going to be giving any more commands—on this earth anyway.

But the two traveling companions had hardly caught their breaths when they both heard the noise at the same instant. The sounds of dozens of men coming from the village. Sticks and blades danced around in the dawn light as they ran down the road toward the burning drug factory. Stone hefted both pistols in his hands and rose as the dog turned, snorted a few times to get its macho going—since it knew they weren't coming out of what was going to happen next. The dog was no fool. There were too many.

"Shit," Stone muttered through still-chattering teeth. He didn't feel like dying today. He at least would have liked to have been completely off the damn drugs. Then he could head into the next world with full consciousness. There was something about dying with a stinking headache and pains in every joint in your body, that just wasn't how he wanted to go. Not that he had particularly wanted to go any fucking way. But then, death didn't give a shit about his likes or dislikes.

The thirty or so upper echelon of the Perfect Aura cult grew ashen-faced as they drew closer. The elephant that had carried the Guru was down. And the huge puddle of blood oozing out from its body with a few of the Guru's rings and jewelry mixed in with it didn't look too promising.

"You killed him," one of them with dark gray robe and various insignia on him indicating a top commander said incredulously. "You killed the Guru."

"Correction," Stone said, wanting to give credit where credit was due. "The elephant killed the Guru."

"But—you—you killed the elephant," the cult officer said, his face turning redder by the second.

"Correction," Stone said, wanting to give credit where credit was due, "the dog killed the elephant." Excaliber glanced up at Stone and stepped a foot or two away, wondering momentarily just who the traitor was. "Of course he's my dog. So if you want to mess with him, you'll have to deal with me first."

"Oh, we will deal with both of you," the Guru's Chief of Arms said as he motioned with his hands for the robed attackers to spread out. And they did so fast, before Stone had a chance to fire. Suddenly they were rushing off in every direction, trying to outflank him from 360 degrees. Stone opened up with the 9mm, spraying a group that was coming in fast at three o'clock. Three of them fell as the slugs criss-crossed over their chests. But they were coming in from everywhere. Excaliber leaped up at one who charged in with

some kind of long machete. He thought he had the dog clear
in his reach and swung the blade down. But suddenly the
animal was right up over it and soaring into his head. The pit
bull chomped down hard right on the center of the man's
face. Nose, lips, eyes, everything—all sort of mushed up
and squirted out between the dog's jaws. Then the fighting
canine spat it all out and turned ready to take on the next
bastard dumb enough to die.

Two of them leapt up at Stone from behind him, just
suddenly there. He got one with the 9mm, sending him flying backward with his whole front opened up as if he was on
medical display. But the second one was able to swing down
the infernal staff that the bastards carried and caught Stone a
good one right on the side of the head. He felt himself going
down—but not out. And even as he hit the ground he managed to bring up the Ruger .44 in a slow arc. The robed
attacker dropped to one knee and was bringing the end of his
stick down toward Stone's nose ready to crush everything
there into paste. But at the last possible instant Stone managed to throw a little extra zing into his arm and the pistol
suddenly flew up and found the target. He squeezed hard,
and the Perfect Aura of the attacker wasn't so perfect anymore, what with a hole the size of a saucer suddenly appear-
ing where his nose had been. Blood exploded out over Stone
as the force of the blast threw the screaming man backward,
where he flopped around like a chicken with its head lopped
off.

Stone rolled over just as an ax descended, and he was
able to take the attacker down with a leg grab, twisting him
to the ground. As the brown-robed man hit the dirt, Stone
slammed the butt end of the .44 right into the fat gut and
pulled twice. The whole backbone exploded out, followed
by much of the digestive system and that day's food as well.
Stone kicked himself free even as the dying eyes spun
around in the white face like cherries in a slot machine. He
jumped to his feet and nearly went over instantly, as he was
still only at about forty percent of fighting ability—which

was not exactly the state to be in in the middle of a full-scale fucking war.

Stone glanced over to the right about ten yards off, where three man lay writhing in crazy patterns on the dirt, blood coming from faces, stomachs, throats. And even as he watched, another attacker came in. The dog feinted to the right and then flew in from the left, slamming his jaws around the wrist of the hand that was carrying a macelike object. Again the animal's razor-sharp jaws did their thing. The hand, holding the club and all, was torn free from the arm that had carried it around for about thirty-six years. The man ran off, blood spurting from his severed wrist, as Excaliber stood there, panting heavily, holding the hand, club and all, in his jaws as he waited for the next asshole.

Stone knew they were both putting up a valiant, incredible fight, considering their states. But it was all going to be in vain. That he had no illusions about. For there were more of the bastards coming all the time. For every one they took out, two more appeared. He'd run out of bullets and the dog would run out of fucking teeth before they took out half of these. Still they fought on. They had no choice. They pulled in closer together, protecting their backs until they were just inches apart, facing off the advancing cultees with murder in their eyes. Stone turned to the mutt, keeping one eye cocked on the attackers.

"Sorry, boy, you don't deserve to go out like this. But— you done good, dog, real fucking good." The pit bull barked twice as if to say ditto. And a twisted smile crossed Stone's face even as he saw that he was down to his last few rounds. Between the two of them they'd already destroyed the fucking place. Taken out its drug supply—and its Guru. All things considered, Stone could almost die happy. Almost. The cultees closed in.

Suddenly there was a strange noise like singing or chanting, and they all seemed to freeze in their tracks. Every face turned to see what the hell the commotion was all about. And coming over the hill Stone saw what was just about the best fucking thing he had ever laid eyes on in his life. The Broken Ones—and they were armed and singing.

"God bless America, land of the free/ Stand beside her and Guide her/ With the light from night from above."

"From the mountains . . ."

Stone joined in under his breath as a real smile crossed his face. He hadn't sung it in a long time. And maybe there was no more America . . . but *these* bastards were singing it—and they were coming to save his damn ass, so Stone sang along, louder, and then louder. And in his heart he almost felt that there was a country again, a nation where the little guy was protected instead of squashed and broken by every two-bit hoodlum, warlord, or guru who deigned to take over a chunk of the ol' U.S. of A.

Riding in the front of the two dozen or so Broken Ones, who hobbled along with broken bodies but unbroken spirit in their hearts, was Smythe on Stone's Harley. He had a wide grin on his half-toothed mouth. And though the Harley was wobbling from side to side, he was keeping the damn thing up. He looked proud as a man can be, both for himself and for the fact that they had all come. And he and Stone caught each other's glances even from the hundred feet or so that parted them and they both knew that it was a feat of mythical proportions. That these battered and torn men, with half their brains gone, should somehow find it in their souls to rise and fight back. That was what it was all about. And it made Stone suddenly feel filled with an invincible strength. And he knew that somehow they were going to make it.

The cult officers, who had been enjoying some pretty good odds against Stone and the dog, suddenly seemed a lot less sure about the mini-army of the brain-broken men. They knew who they were. They had seen them all be broken— too far—and sent out into the wilds to die. It was all too much for them. The Guru dead . . . And now these ex-pods who should be dead returning with weapons in their hands. Their entire universe was turning upside down.

Suddenly, with croaking but spirited rebel yells the Broken Ones charged in, or charged as fast as men with not everything all there can charge. Still, it was the thought that counted. They tore into the confused cultees with their homemade weapons—branches with nails driven through them, clubs with hand-sharpened rocks lashed down to their tops, spears made from rusted kitchen knives. But lots of things will kill. Human flesh is terribly penetrable. Death doesn't care how tacky is the implement used to bring it new souls.

TWENTY-FOUR

Stone fired his last few rounds and then used the pistols as clubs, smashing his way toward the fighting Broken Ones. With the pit bull covering his flank, they reached them within a few seconds. Stone put his arm on Smythe's shoulder.

"You just saved my fucking ass, pal," Stone said through a grimacing mouth. One of the robed attackers had gotten a good slice on his shoulder and he was just starting to feel it.

"You saved *our* asses, Stone," Smythe said, beaming like a kid with a new toy at the fact that he'd been able to lead this squad of dead men into battle. To be a man is the hardest thing to attain.

"You think you can handle these bastards?" Stone asked as Smythe got up from the seat so Stone could get on.

"No trouble, mister," Smythe said with a firm look. "The hard part was getting ourselves human again. The rest is easy."

"Thanks. I gotta check out something right away. I'll be back in a few minutes." Smythe turned and ran across the street, where fierce hand-to-hand was going on everywhere. Men were collapsed in struggling heaps, and bodies covered with red lay all around. It was a nasty fight. Stone whistled and the dog flew up onto the back seat, its tail wagging for the first time since it had been in the damn place. The seat was its security blanket, and it pressed down flat against it, clamping all four legs around it like a bank robber around money. It was never letting go. Stone twisted the accelerator and the Harley screamed out its power, rolling over two dead cultees that squished like blood-filled waterbeds beneath his wheels.

He tore ass down the road toward town as the fire from the Nectar factory spat out an acrid smoke that was already filling the air for hundreds of yards and heading rapidly toward the main part of town. There was pandemonium everywhere, with robed figures running up and down the streets, voices shouting. But no one seemed to know quite what to do. The whole scene was unorganized, already disintegrating into anarchy. Stone had nothing against most of the cultees—he had just been one himself. But he wasn't letting anyone try to kill him, either. So, when a few overaggressive robed figures came tearing toward the bike from the side of the street, Stone sprayed them with a burst from the .50-caliber on the front of the bike. Three robes spouted blood and they spun back like tops.

The bike shot down the main street, accelerating every yard. Figures dove out of the way as the roaring cycle rocketed like a black panther through the center of town. It took Stone only a minute to reach the palace. He remembered how it had seemed like the very house of God to his moronic brain just a day or so before. How he had been in awe of the palace and couldn't even look at it when he drew near. That wasn't quite the case now.

The four guards at the front door weren't ready for what came at them out of the dawn—a cruiserweight Harley pouring smoke from its pipes at the superacceleration Stone was pushing it to. They barely had time to get their weapons to half-staff before the blurred vehicle opened up with a hailstorm of slugs. Four bodies went dancing around in a ballroom of blood before they slipped right into the grave.

Stone didn't wait around for any parting words. Holding his head down, he screamed.

"Duck, dog, duck!" Which was simple but clear advice. The bike slammed right into the thick wooden doors. And tore them off their rusting hinges. The Harley came barreling into the main lobby of the late Guru's palatial retreat. There was wealth everywhere—carpets, tapestries, huge oil paintings—all stolen from nearby museums, taken from the possessions of those whose brains had been taken over. But Stone wasn't on the museum tour. For another bunch of Elite Guards opened up from various hiding places around the big marble-pillared lobby. Stone was sure April was on the second floor; that was where the harem was rumored to be.

He saw wide, curving stairs to the left and wheeled the bike around, slowing to about thirty miles per hour. He was barely in control, so tight was the turn. It skimmed and shimmied all around the marble floor and went right over the back of a man who had been hiding behind a chair. His spine cracked like a chicken bone at Sunday dinner. Slugs poured out from everywhere, like murderous hands trying to squeeze his skull. But Stone reached the bottom of the wide stone staircase and wheeled the bike around again. The moment the front wheel hit the bottom step he turned the throttle to full and bent all the way forward. The motorcycle shot up the stairs as if there was gold at the top as slugs whizzed all around it, unable to get a bead on the two riders.

The ride was like going through rapids, and both Stone and the pit bull were bounced around as though they were in an earthquake. But somehow they hung on, and within two seconds were at the second-floor landing. More guards awaited them at the far end of the floor, and Stone headed straight toward them, figuring where there were guards there was something to guard. It was hardly fair—to them. As they kneeled down and lifted their Nato 7.2mm assault rifles, Stone merely moved his thumb a half an inch to the left and pressed hard. And fifteen slugs shot out of the smoking barrel mounted on the front wheel. About half of them seemed to take a liking to the one on the left, the other the guy on the right. In any case, it hardly mattered. For when they had finished tearing through pounds of flesh, both men were not much more than yesterday's leftovers which any self-respecting alleycat wouldn't touch. They slid along the marble floor like hockey pucks and hit the back wall, where they spattered blood all over the golden floor-to-ceiling curtains.

Stone slowed the bike to a near stop at the end of the hall, turned it with one leg down, and then accelerated again, slamming right into two oak doors, which flew back against the inside wall like drums crashing at the end of a Wagner symphony. The bike flew inside, knocking over tables, chairs, all kinds of stuff, finally slamming into a wall, where Stone and traveling dog went flying off the vehicle and right into the plaster surface in a most painful manner.

The smoke and dust and plaster dust had hardly cleared when Stone heard a dry high-pitched cackling sound coming from the far side of the room. He wiped his eyes free of the dust that was floating around them and, coughing a few times, ripped his Ruger .44 from its holster and turned to see what God had wrought.

And he could hardly believe his eyes. For just twenty feet away from him, in between the Transformer on his left and April on the right, was the Dwarf, the hideous armless and legless criminal monstrosity who traveled in a machine-gun-equipped mobile wheelchair. Stone had killed the wretched little egg man months before. He had thrown the bastard from a twelve-story building. It was impossible. Stone's face must have showed his confusion. For the Dwarf laughed louder and shook its head from side to side like a basketball trying to come free and find a basket.

"What are the thoughts of the mindless?" he asked in his inevitable Zen Koan of death.

"Blackness," Stone answered, slowly raising his hand in

the shadows and smoke. "I should know. I've just been there."

"Oh, Stone, it's all just too funny," the Dwarf shrieked in that high-pitched voice that Stone couldn't stand, like a puppet that had gone psycho. But it didn't look too funny to Stone—not with his sister standing there with a look as dead as rock on her face. And on the other side of the war wheelchair—the Transformer, with his leathery dead face and glowing red eyes burning from within the black hood. It was quite a crew. Although Stone supposed that with the blood-coated dog by his side, the two of them didn't look a hell of a lot better.

"What do you want?" Stone asked, holding his gun at a slight tilt, ready to take out either of them at any moment. But there was something up—it wasn't as simple as it appeared. No way. Stone knew the Dwarf. He had already escaped certain death several times. Stone's senses, even in the midst of his drug withdrawal, were on full alert as he scanned around wildly looking for the trap.

"You're wondering how I survived the fall," the Dwarf said, pushing a button with one of his stumps. The Dwarf, who resembled nothing so much as a huge pasty-white egg with cancerous growths coming out a few inches where arms and legs should be, had a little bit of mobility with the pointed stumps of red flesh that protruded from the shoulders. And with these it could poke at a whole array of buttons and dials all around the side of its high-tech motorized wheelchair. "I fell into water. A swimming pool, Stone. You should have looked."

"Yeah, I sure should have," Stone whispered bitterly. "What do you want, Dwarf?" he asked, wondering if he and April had just run out of time.

"What does a man with everything want?" The Dwarf laughed in his high voice, with such shrieking tonalities that it hurt Stone's ears. Even the dog let out a little howl, as it heard the higher frequencies with even greater acuity—and it didn't like what it heard one bit.

"He wants it all," Stone answered with a grunt.

"Exactly. Right again, aren't you? He wants all. So there is nothing you can offer to bargain with me, foolish man. I hold all the cards." At the word *cards* as if on prearranged signal, the ceiling right above Stone suddenly opened up and a steel cable net came flying down, ballooning out over both man and dog. Stone had his hands full—for coming right behind the net were eight guys who looked as if they had been lifting cows before breakfast. But he had caveman equalizers of his own. He ripped both pistols up and fired. And kept firing. The slugs tore through the steel netting, severing a whole section to the side of him—and taking out four of the attackers.

As the smoke swirled all around him, Stone rolled through the bullet-created opening with the pit bull right on his heels. They came out fighting, Stone slamming the butt of his Ruger right into a nose as the pit bull took out a kneecap in one bloody bite and the stricken leg collapsed like a broken Tinkertoy. Stone whipped his glance across the room, but to his horror the Dwarf was already rolling off out a door he hadn't seen—as two hoods pulled April along. Not that was she resistant. She was as docile as a cow being led to slaughter. Who wouldn't be with all the quarts of junk she had floating around in her bloodstream?

Suddenly the Transformer jumped right in his path, blocking Stone from going on. From out of his robe the hands pulled long daggers, which he twirled around fast, showing Stone what he could do.

"You die now," the mechanical voice croaked out from within the hood. "You and your fucking dog." He threw one of the knives fast, and it slammed right into Excaliber's chest before the animal could even move. Stone looked with horror as he saw the blade go in and the dog go down. Instantly the other hand whipped out and the knife whizzed straight at Stone's throat. Only the fact that he had been leaning over forward to see the dog saved his life, as the throwing dagger missed his neck by an inch and flew past, sticking into one of the Transformer's own elite bodyguards who had been sneaking up on Stone with maces in hand.

But even as Stone ripped his pistols up to get a sight on the Transformer, two more knives appeared in the High Priest's hands and they flew out. Both hit their targets—Stone's hands. One glanced off his left hand, leaving a long gouge along the top. The other dug right into the back of the hand and went through it. The result was just what the Transformer wanted—Stone dropped his guns and was suddenly completely vulnerable.

He reached over with his gouged hand and ripped the blade from the other. But even as he tried to hold the knife with the gouged hand, it slipped out. The fingers weren't quite working right. Transformer was closing in on him fast, wanting to do it by hand now, slashing forward into Stone's chest and face. Stone barely jumped out of the way as the black-robed figure moved forward with lightning speed. He knew one more charge, and—

And he was right. For the Transformer suddenly stabbed with a lunge and Stone felt the point of the blade rip right into his chest. The bones of his ribs stopped it from slipping through to his heart, but as he grimaced with pain Stone was flung backward by the sheer force of the blow. He fell onto a rug and the whole thing slid a few yards along the floor. But it was all over. He had nothing. No more tricks. The Transformer sprinted over and stood above him, straddling Stone with both legs. He raised his arms up high, each hand holding one of the long daggers—like a matador about to spear a bull. Stone suddenly realized that he was clutching the leg of a chair he had somehow grabbed as he fell. With a burst of strength from the very far reaches of his soul, he pulled hard. The leg snapped about two feet up from the floor, and he whipped the jagged piece around and up.

The Transformer laughed a hollow robotic laugh and came down, both knives gleaming like death's eyes. Stone thrust up with the chair leg—and hit something. And he continued to push and push, even as his stabbed hands screamed out for mercy. The stake slammed beneath the robe and right up into the lower rib cage of the Transformer. In an instant it had slid up a foot and a half, ripping through both lungs, cutting his heart in two. And as Stone madly thrust on, looking directly into the ugly death face, the glowing red eyes, the Transformer suddenly let out with an unearthly scream. The stake pushed on, and suddenly the attacker couldn't scream at all. For the wooden point of the jagged chair leg emerged from his mouth coated in red.

Stone fell back and released the wood as the pierced Transformer staggered backward, his whole insides, heart, throat, completely obliterated. He was dead already; he just didn't know it. But as he stumbled backward his feet caught on a carpet and the High Priest of the Perfect Aura toppled over onto his back, where the arms snapped around like snakes with jolts of electricity being fed into their tails. Stone picked up one of the fallen blades and prepared to slam it into the Transformer's brain if necessary. But he was dead. As dead as a man could get with a wooden chair leg going nearly three feet through him.

And Stone saw as well, as the hood flew off the leather head, that it was a mask, hanging from the face. The Transformer was no supernatural being. His red eyes were bulbs, the corpselike features all latex. And beneath it all, just one ugly-looking mug who looked like he could have been Al Capone's brother, but sure as hell wasn't a demon from the netherworlds.

Not that his identity mattered. Stone rose to both legs, his hands hanging at his side while they dripped little rivulets of blood down onto the carpet. He stumbled to the window—and saw them. The Dwarf and April being loaded into the back of a big diesel truck. And even as he watched, the back of the thing was closed up. With a big puff of smoke from the diesel stack on the front cabin, the truck was off. And he knew that in the state he was in, there was no way in hell he was going to catch it. He could hardly walk, let alone drive. He lifted his hands.

They looked like shit, covered with so much red it was hard to tell just what the damage was.

But the dog had gotten it worse. It wasn't moving, just lying there with the damn knife coming right out of its chest. Stone got down on one trembling knee and reached down and pulled the knife free. There was a little whimper, but the canine's eyes didn't even open. He knew the dog was tough. He had never seen it go completely out. Christ, things just got worse and worse. No matter what, it seemed he couldn't escape the fires—or those who dared stand with him.

TWENTY-FIVE

Stone drove the Harley back to the battle scene on the main street. He moved slowly so as not to dislodge the pit bull, which he had tied down on a blanket behind him. It wasn't moving. He came to a stop and looked around at the bodies strewn everywhere. Most of them were robed. Suddenly there was motion from a door, and as Stone reached toward the trigger for the .50-caliber he saw that it was Smythe. The leader of the Broken Ones walked over to him, letting the pistol in his right hand dangle loosely.

"We done it. We fucking done it," he said, amazed. "It don't make me feel too good, though, I'll tell you. Ain't seen this many bodies in my life. A lot of them's my crew —but it had to be done and we done it. Reclaimed our damn land, our farms and homes, from these murderers." Stone looked around. The upper echelon of the cult were either dead or dying. The rest had fled into the woods. Without the brains of the cult, there was nothing. Already the cultees were starting to walk around the town with puzzled expressions on their faces. They were all starting to come off the Golden Nectar and couldn't even walk quite right, dragging their legs, making moaning and howling sounds from all around the camp. It was a mess, to say the least.

"See the bastards got your dog," Smythe said, looking

down at Excaliber as Stone wearily dismounted. The bandages he had taken from the med supplies and wrapped around his hands with his teeth were bleeding through again. But the main flow had stopped, less than a third of what it had been just minutes before. He wasn't going to die—not from this anyway. Even if he might want to.

"He's still alive. But for how long I don't know," Stone said so softly he could hardly be heard.

"That's a shame, a damn shame. I seen that dog fighting right alongside you out there. Damn brave animal." Suddenly the man snapped his fingers. "Wait a second—Walt was a doctor. Maybe he could do something. We got access to medical supplies now. I think he came through it all okay —I seen him just a few minutes ago." Smythe whistled hard, and after a minute or so, they got Walt to come round. Stone looked at the fellow, not hoping for much. The fellow was emaciated, his chest sunken in, his face a mass of sores and oozing stuff. Yet within the eyes Stone saw a spark of real intelligence. Fighting back had brought them back to themselves. Had at least put them in the right direction.

"What do you think?" Smythe said, pointing at the dog. "Can you do anything?"

"Naw . . . I ain't practiced for years." The man laughed, putting up his hands. But his curiosity got the better of him and he leaned over the animal, putting his ear to the furred chest, where he listened for a few seconds and then stood up again. "Well, I don't know. There's still a heartbeat. But it's weak, and he needs to be cut open and given a—a heart operation. Stitched up and everything—"

"Do it!" Stone said in a pained whisper. "Just do it. If he dies, I won't blame you. He's going to die anyway, so . . ." Stone and the would-be doctor carried the animal a few blocks to the med building, where some of the cultees were walking around bumping into walls. They weren't even threats anymore, more dangers to themselves as they broke their noses and smashed their teeth out banging into things. The damn mindless wonders didn't know what the hell they were doing or even that they were in bodies—flesh and blood that could be hurt.

Inside, the doctor put Excaliber up on a sterile operating table and then gathered various medical supplies—scalpels, alcohol. Stone could hardly bear to watch as Excaliber's fur was cut open. But he had to stay—to be there for the animal that had been there for him. Imagine attacking a fucking elephant. He shook his head from side to side. It only took the doctor about an hour. He cut right into the chest, poked around, saw that part of the heart itself had been ruptured—and actually sewed it up again, using self-dissolving gut cord. Then he sutured the hide closed again. Needles were put into arteries of the dog's armpits and dripping fluid was fed into them from IV bags that hung suspended on mobile racks on each side of the hardly breathing animal.

"I've given him massive amounts of antibiotics, and also a heart stimulator to make sure he doesn't conk out. We'll keep him in here, I guess, so I can keep feeding the stuff into him intravenously. Now, let me take a look at you," he said. Before Stone could protest, he grabbed Stone's hands and laid them down on the table, swabbing them off with alcohol.

"Ah, not too bad," he said after examining them for a minute. He bandaged up the stab wound, which had cleanly penetrated the hand but hadn't severed any arteries or muscles. The other gash required twenty stitches, then a bandage wrapped all the way around the hand a number of times to keep it from getting infected. Stone looked like a caricature of a man who had been poking his hands into things he shouldn't—a beehive or something.

"Well, I sure appreciate your efforts," Stone said as the two of them walked out to the front of the place and stood out on the sidewalk. Blocks off the drug factory burned, but the wind at least had shifted, so the acrid smoke was blowing off in the opposite direction. Let it all burn, Stone thought bitterly as he watched. Let the drugs burn until there isn't a molecule of them left. Until they can't poison one more human brain.

"What do you think, Doc? Tell me the truth?" Stone said after several minutes of silence.

"I really don't know, mister. I'll be honest with you," Walter replied. "I've done my best. I think I actually did all the right things. At least I didn't kill him. Now it's up to the dog's inherent strength—and the ability of the heart to withstand the shock and not go into cardiac arrest. But I'll stand by him. I owe you—we all owe you—that much."

"Well, I'll keep you company," Stone said, looking down the street as some of the Broken Ones started spontaneously dancing as they hooked arms and jumped around. They sure as hell didn't look broken anymore. "We'll see how he is tomorrow. And then if he's dead, I'll bury the brave little bastard. And if he's alive, well, then he's off for one more fucking descent into hell. 'Cause that's where I'm heading. I've got a date with a psycho dwarf. And only one of us is coming out alive."

The wounded were being dragged down the street. Of the twenty-four Broken Ones who had begun the attack, ten had died. Another six were wounded, some with their guts hanging out, painting a highway line down the middle of the street. They dragged them right up the three steps that led to where Stone and Doc Walter were standing, and looked at him imploringly.

"But I can't," he said, stepping back in horror at the heavy wounds. "I can't promise that I won't—won't kill them."

"You didn't do in the dog," Stone commented dryly as the sun rose like a yellow boil on the face of the world, skulking above the trees. "Face it man, you're the new doctor here in this hellhole. And Smythe here is the new mayor." Both men looked around in utter terror. It seemed to frighten them a lot more than the actual battle had. "Hey, there's no choice about it," Stone went on as they began dragging the wounded inside. "You're the builders of this town. The makers. You're the ones who can bring it out of the poison and horror that have occurred here, and into something human and decent. Maybe even add a little light to this barbaric and dying country. It's *me*—I'm the one who can't rest, who can't ever stay in one place. Until I find her, I have no home."